NEVER WICKED

An Anthology of Short Stories
in support of
The Mayhew Animal Home

Published by: We Made This Publishing Limited
12 Stephen Mews, London
W1T 1AH
www.museability.com

ISBN: 978-0-9568763-0-0

Cover Image: © Josephine Dexter 2011, from original artwork commissioned specifically for this book

Design and Layout by Ruggiero Campopiano at Picsoul
www.picsoul.com

Printed by: MPG-Biddles Limited, Norfolk www.mpg-biddles.co.uk

Typeset: Mangal 14pt (Titles); Palatino Linotype 10pt (copyrights/acknowledgements); Constantia 10pt (text)

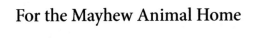For the Mayhew Animal Home

"It is much easier to show compassion to animals.
They are never wicked."

Haile Selassie - Ethiopian Statesman and Emperor of Ethiopia from 1930
to 1974, 1892 - 1975

Table of Contents

Forward.. *viii*

Percy by Neil Andrew Taylor... 1

Custody by Amy Blyth.. 5

The Pageant by Angela Songui.. 17

Rat Love by Amarpreet Basi... 25

Bouncing Silhouettes by Josephine Dexter....................... 31

The Age of the Rat by Amy Blyth....................................... 45

Three Twats and a Dog Turd by WTA Mackewn............ 49

Henrietta and the Crow by Christina Thompson............. 59

Wave Goodbye by Rebecca Jenkins..................................... 69

A Lovers Tale by Angela Songui.. 81

Acknowledgements.. 85

Author Biographies.. 87

FORWARD

When I was a little girl I was hooked on shows like *Untamed World* and *Mutual of Omaha's Wild Kingdom*.

The epic 'struggle' for survival held a bizarre fascination and romance for me.

Yes, I was one strange child... but although I could easily be led to 'feel' for these animals, I was always a bit mystified by our own choices when it came to investing these creatures and their day-to-day realities with human emotion.

Why did we always opt for a negative viewpoint?

Was this really going to expand my understanding of the human condition or simply place human values on a world that doesn't work in the same way?

It seemed, and still seems, far too easy for us to disallow an animal a 'soul' and yet invest its everyday actions with attitudes designed to suit our own version of The Epic Struggle without really addressing the contradictions.

For instance:

Lion alone on rock = majestic, kingly

Lion chasing gazelle = dominance, oppression – pitting the poor gazelle/victim against the bad lion/bully

... followed by the inevitable implication: 'Well, kids, that is how life works', as if this granted a licence to our own poor behaviour.

As I stood outside the place where our Writers' Group meets, thinking these thoughts and watching folk down their drinks at the pub next door, I began also to ponder ways in which artists and writers could produce some challenging work as well as some charitable 'good.' The idea of creating a 'bespoke' collection of tales crafted to attract a fresh set of supporters for a worthy cause would be a great exercise for the group and our abilities. My target charity: The Mayhew Animal Home.

Our theme is broad and the content has proven to be as unique as each individual contributing to the project. Our collective goals are simple: to provide The Mayhew with a new format of fundraising material created specifically for their organisation; to raise funds and awareness of this wonderful charity; to publish our work independently and benefit collectively from the 'real-world of publishing' experience (no, we are NOT making money from this project - all profits from sales benefit The Mayhew Animal Home only). We invite you to imagine the world through luminous eyes, and take note that our creature-companion's presence, however slight, holds a mirror up to our deepest thoughts and desires.

And of course, we hope you enjoy.

Angela Songui - Project Director

"Animals are such agreeable friends - they ask no questions, they pass no criticisms."

George Eliot – novelist, journalist, 1819 - 1880

PERCY
Neil Andrew Taylor

In my determination to get down south I turned to my last, but immediate hope. There I was, a grown man with a piggy bank. Large, white, bought from Habitat. A noble pig with a smiling face and a huge rubber stopper near its arse where the money could be retrieved from. It was lucky it wasn't in a thousand pieces, but you never know when you might need a piggy bank again. I mused the symbolism of the fact. In my youth all the images of piggy banks I'd seen had been geared to showing me that piggy banks were designed to be smashed open. With a hammer. Or a chair leg. Or a fist. But it had to be smashed. I was never, ever, shown a pig with a bung up its bum.

Of course! Those images, nursery stories, children's books, cartoons, adverts, were designed to show that once you'd broken into your savings your pig was smashed forever, never to be repaired. You couldn't have both pig, which, presumably, you'd grown emotionally attached to and savings, which, presumably, you'd also grown emotionally attached to! The raiding of your savings was a desperate act to be discouraged and thus promote thrift. Savings were a Victorian virtue. Once you had broken your financial pact with the pig there was no way back. It was a capitalist pig, there to teach you a lesson in hard economics the china way.

But there was the small matter of getting out of the house, which was rapidly turning into a coffin. You'll never get a shag sitting at home watching the telly.

High Definition doesn't get you laid.

Suddenly I relished the thought of smashing my pig open. I ran down to the cellar, rummaged in my tool box and retrieved a hammer.

Like the old tool-shop joke about bastard files, this was a fuck-off hammer, mean and weighty, a Thor-like instrument of fiscal retribution ready to smash into a kiln-fired Scrooge that was beginning to look like Lee Van Cleef. Adios amigo! I ran back upstairs. Now, hammer in one hand, porcelain pork in the other I raised that hickory shafted reminder of who's boss way on high and in one swift movement brought it crashing down past Percy's left ear.

I couldn't do it. Not to Percy. He'd been steadfast. Loyal. He'd cheerfully guarded his coins for my rainy day.

Instead I whipped out the stopper and shoved my fingers right up his rectum and started waggling them about desperately trying to feel for any long lost fivers I might have shoved in there from the top end. Then, there, at the very tips of my fingers was the rustle of paper. One, maybe two notes. With a little extra leverage against Percy's corkscrew tail I could just...just ...YES!!!!!!!!!!!!!!!!! Out popped a tenner!!! When had I put that in there? Who gives a shit? I could afford a bus ticket!

"Being asked what animal you'd like to be is a trick question; you're already an animal."

Douglas Coupland – novelist, 1961

CUSTODY
Amy Blyth

"What time did you get in last night?"

Harry jumps at the sound of Jasmine's voice and tries woozily to sit up, but the sofa seems to be swaying beneath him. His stomach lurches, sending last night's lager sloshing against the insides of his gut. Bracing his head with one hand Harry swivels it in Jasmine's direction; framed in the lounge doorway she stands with her arms crossed over her chest, hair tied back severely, her perfectly painted cherry lips set in a tight line.

"No idea," he mumbles, trying to recall what exactly *had* happened last night. He remembers sitting in the Nag's Head with Ian, the rugby on the new widescreen TV, lagers lined up on the sticky bar, and, hang on - were there whisky shots in there too? A hazy memory of Ian asking him about Jasmine surfaces, followed by some rambling self-pitying speech; tears cried into Ian's best football shirt. *There are other ways - doctors can do wonders now y'know,* his friend had told him.

"Well, I'll tell you what time it was shall I?" Jasmine says, interrupting his thoughts. She is moving around the coffee table now, her high heels clattering painfully on the laminate floor. She yanks open the curtains with such ferocity that the wooden rail shakes. "Four o'clock Harry – that's what time you got in. What in hell were you doing till then? No – scrap that – I don't even want to know."

Harry's brain pulses sickeningly against his skull, irritation rising in his throat as he watches Jasmine noisily tidying the lounge. Even first thing on a Saturday morning she is infuriatingly faultless; fragrant, groomed, every inch of her slender body radiating smug perfection. As if he doesn't feel enough of a failure.

"You look disgusting," she says, as if she's seeing Harry for the first time. Her nose wrinkles as she notices the film of beer-scented sweat glistening on his forehead - his face the colour of thin custard.

"Yep, that's me - your disgusting, useless husband. Why do you bother?" Harry's voice is quiet now and he fears that tears are lurking behind his bloodshot eyes.

"Sometimes I wonder - I'm sick of you out every night, I only see you when you're drunk, or hung over..."

"Well, what do you expect me to do?" he interrupts, "You don't want me here – all I am is one big disappointment."

"Stop with the self-pity, it's pathetic," Jasmine snarls, twisting her wedding ring between her fingers.

"How can I when you so obviously blame me for the baby..."

"Don't you dare," she says, raising one hand, palm up towards him, as if she's halting traffic.

"Well it's true, you do blame me, don't you?" he challenges. Jasmine doesn't reply and as the seconds pass the silence thickens the air.

"Maybe I do," she whispers finally. Harry opens and closes his mouth slowly, stung by her words. "You asked for it Harry – so here it is," there is nothing in her voice, no sadness, no regret – only exasperation.

"Maybe I should leave then..." It's a half question and he waits for her to respond, to take it back, even though he knows nothing can change the truth.

"Maybe you should."

Harry can't look at her as he turns to the lounge door, tears finally clouding his vision. He stops dead with his hand on the doorknob.

"What about Jasper?" he asks suddenly, turning to face her.

"What about him? You don't think you're taking him with you?" she scrunches her face in sheer disbelief.

"Why not?" he answers, indignant now, "He's mine just as much as he is yours."

Jasmine shakes her head incredulously.

"You're not taking him Harry, no way."
"We'll see about that."

Harry throws open the lounge door, stomping down the hall to the kitchen.

"Jasper," he calls, "Come here Jasper..."

Jasmine rushes up the stairs in search of Jasper, ponytail bouncing behind her.

"Jasper," they both cry, jostling for position in the upstairs landing.

Harry throws open one door whilst Jasmine searches their bedroom. Empty.
She turns to face Harry, her face pale and disbelieving:

"Where's he gone?"

-

Jasper eases himself from under the bed, pads softly down the stairs. He glances towards the lounge door as he hurries past, wincing at the sound of their raised voices. The back door is open a crack and he nudges it gently with his nose; the air is cold, the pavement frosty beneath his feet as he trots around the side of the house. Jasper stops dead when he notices it – he hesitates for only a second before bolting through the open gate.

-

"Great, you idiot, you left the damn gate open," Jasmine is pulling on her jacket, feeling for her car keys as she runs down the garden path.
"I didn't!" Harry protests.

She whirls round angrily, one finger pointed at his chest.

"At least I don't think I did..."
"And you really think you're capable of looking after Jasper? Get real," she shouts, pulling open the car door.

Harry moves to the passenger door, glancing up and down the road.

"What do you think you're doing?" she asks, as Harry plonks down in the car seat, yanking the belt round him.

"Helping you look for Jasper -"

"I don't think so."

"Oh shut up Jasmine, I'm coming with you," he snaps.

Jasmine exhales loudly, then, resigning herself to his presence, she starts the engine.

"Just keep your mouth shut and your eyes peeled," she warns.

-

Jasmine resists the urge to stop the car, to boot her husband out. The very feel of him sat next to her, the heat and stench of his unwashed body infuriates her beyond belief. As she swerves away from the house she imagines leaving Harry right here on the pavement, finding Jasper and then just driving, away from him, away from all of this. It has become a familiar fantasy; one that plays over in her head as she sits night after night alone, waiting for Harry to get home from god knows where, with only Jasper for company. Her favourite thing is to imagine herself a year from now, in a new home, with a new man. In her mind he's tall and solid, someone who brings her cups of tea, who talks to her and makes her laugh. Someone who always remembers to put away his clothes, to unload the dishwasher, to kiss her every morning before she leaves for work. Is that so difficult?

It's at this point that she always gets carried away; starts imagining how her body would meld so perfectly with this stranger's, how they'd connect in exactly the right way, how her stomach would swell with the one thing she craved more than anything else – a baby. Then the stranger's face comes into focus and she realises it's Harry she's seeing – only a younger version of him. It's the Harry she met at university; the one who taught her how to drive and helped her revise for her exams; the one she married; the one who doesn't seem to exist anymore. The one who can never give her what she most needs.

Jasmine stares at the road ahead, trying to force her mind back to the present. Jasper could be anywhere – it's so cold – he shouldn't be out here alone. Even though they've lived in this area five years, it looks unfamiliar to her now, every turning, every driveway; every field they pass presents another possibility. Had Jasper turned left? Or right? Or ran straight across the road without looking? She had always been so careful with the gate and Jasper had never run away before. There *had* been that one time he'd gone missing in the woods though, she'd forgotten about it till now. When was that? *It was New Year's Day,* she thinks, *not long after we adopted him.* The weather had been like this, frosty and dry, so icy that your breath freezes and the tip of your nose goes numb. That didn't stop Jasper from bolting off the minute they got to the woods though, he was a whirlwind of energy; they had laughed as he galloped away, barking his head off. Jasmine smiles softly at the memory, she can almost feel Harry's gloved hand in hers; can practically see his face as it was then – slightly thinner and less lined. She can still taste his cold tongue against her chattering teeth as he'd turned to kiss her.

And then of course they'd both realised Jasper was missing. God, how they panicked - they called him for almost an hour; their faces scratched from the undergrowth as they searched. And the relief when they finally found him, tail sticking out of the foxhole, still barking madly – he must have been there ages.

Yep, that was Jasper, never one to back down.

-

As he scans the road for Jasper, Harry steals a glance at Jasmine. Her eyes are slightly glazed, unexpectedly the corner of her mouth curls upwards in a ghost of a smile – what is she thinking about? He used to live for Jasmine's smile; in the old days he could always chase one from her eventually, even when she was in her worst moods. Nothing had made Jasmine smile like Jasper had though. When he'd originally decided to get Jasmine a dog, he had thought of getting a poodle or something expensive like a husky – perhaps a Dalmatian. He'd only gone to the animal shelter out of interest, just to take a look - but then he'd spotted Jasper.

He was tiny back then, his white fur interspersed with black spots – and one brown spot over his left eye - as if he was wearing an eye patch. He had pale pink markings on his stomach, like a pig. Despite

9

his miniature size, Harry could tell right away that Jasper had a real attitude, the Jack Russell jumped up at the bars as he approached, yapping ferociously, his little tail stuck out straight behind him. Small but feisty - just like Jasmine. The smile on her face when she set eyes on him – she'd loved Jasper the moment she saw him.

-

Harry notices the way Jasmine bites her lower lip as she peers out the windscreen; a nervous habit she hasn't been able to shake. It's gotten so bad in recent weeks, since she threw away that last pregnancy test, that she's developed a persistent scab. The sight of her chewing reminds Harry of that day – how he came home from work to find Jasmine in bed, Jasper lying next to her. Her eyes were almost swollen shut with sobs, the floor littered with tissues – among them lay the discarded test – it's angry red line staring back at him. Negative.

This time he hadn't been able to comfort her – he couldn't continue promising that they could try again when everything was so clearly falling apart. They'd been trying for two years. Harry had always suspected it was his fault, so when the doctor's report came back, he wasn't surprised to see that *he* was the defective one. How could it ever have been Jasmine? Perfect Jasmine. She doesn't deserve this – but neither does he.

Harry still sees the same sadness in her face, buried beneath the layers of carefully applied foundation, concealer and light-pink blusher. There are delicate lines around her large hazel eyes, so flecked with orange they look ginger. It's her eyes that break Harry's heart the most – when they were happy together Jasmine's eyes were his favourite thing to look at - but now they are the one part of her that won't be covered with powders and creams, the one thing she can't disguise with expensive scents and fabrics. Her eyes reflect sorrow and disappointment back at him, reminding him every second that he's the cause of her pain. He almost can't bear to look at Jasmine anymore; it's easier to turn away.

"Jas," he speaks quietly. She doesn't answer, her gaze intent on the road ahead, sweeping from left to right to check the pavements. "I'm sorry."

Jasmine looks at him from the corner of her eye. "For what? Leaving the gate open like a drunken idiot?" The animosity is still there.

"Yes," he replies with a sigh, "Sorry for that – and sorry that I can't give you what you want."

She shoots him a warning look, but Harry ignores it. This has gone unsaid for too long.

"Jasmine I'm sorry we can't – *I can't* – have a baby. I know how upset, how angry you are that I can't give you that."

She flicks the indicator on with one hand, her opal varnish sparkling in the wintry sunlight.

"What are you doing?" Harry asks, as she pulls over to the side of the road. When she snaps off the engine the silence in the car absorbs everything, the smell of pine air freshener threatening Harry's still delicate stomach.

Jasmine exhales loudly and puts her face in her hands. It's a moment before Harry realises she's crying, softly at first, then great shaking sobs that rack her small body. Harry places his hand on her back warily; his own tears snaking silently down his cheeks. For a moment Jasmine moves to shake him off, before surrendering to his touch as he circles his hand over her back – it reminds him absurdly of the times at university when she'd get too drunk and he'd stand by, rubbing her back as she threw up in the student union toilets.

Finally she sits up and tries to wipe her face with her hands, her makeup is smudged, her skin raw and vulnerable, and Harry realises it's the first time he's seen her like this in weeks, since the last negative pregnancy test.

"I still love you the same, you know that, don't you?" he asks and she turns to face him for the first time. "I married you because I wanted to be with *you* – a baby..."

Jasmine winces at the word, as if he's just thrown something at her. "A baby would be great and you'd be brilliant with a kid, I know you would – I would love a baby Jas. But I love you more. I love you even if it's just you and me – and Jasper."

Jasmine takes a couple of shuddering breaths in and out, trying to compose herself.

"We could try IVF again, or, or we could adopt," says Harry, Ian's words flashing into his mind.
"We've been through this," she sighs, "I want my, *our* child – something that really belongs to us, and what if IVF doesn't work? I can't go through all that again. "
"We'll keep trying," he answers.
"Like we're trying now? Like we've been trying to fix things these last few months you mean?" she asks, "We're falling apart as it is... you never even bother to come home anymore."
"Because all I ever seem to do is upset you, not because I don't want to be at home – I've been stupid," Harry rubs his face with both hands. "We can still work things out, if you think that could be enough for you, Jas?" he whispers.
Jasmine shakes her head wearily. "I don't know yet, Harry. I really don't."

The words run dry and they both sit, staring ahead out the windscreen until Jasmine breaks the silence with a soft chuckle. Harry looks at her in surprise, his eyebrow arched.

"I was thinking 'bout the time we lost him in the woods," Jasmine says, wiping the last of the wetness from her cheeks. She looks at Harry with a smile. "Do you remember his little tail sticking out of the hole?" Harry laughs gently in response. "He was so stubborn! He just wouldn't admit defeat would he?" Jasmine continues, shaking her head in wonderment.
"Yep, he's stubborn alright, just like his owner," Harry says, nudging Jasmine's knee with his hand. He looks at the clock on the dashboard, it's nearly midday. *No wonder Jasper ran off,* he thinks, *he's used to having his walk early on a Saturday morning* – come rain or shine they'd always take the same route – up the road past the newsagents, across the park, round the local woods...
"Hey!" says Harry, jerking upright in his seat.
"What?"
"I think I know where he might be..."

Jasper is shivering in his nest of sticks and leaves. It feels like he's been sat here hours, listening to the sounds of the woods; the animals and birds, the wind in the trees and later the insistent pattering of sleet pecking at the leaves and earth beneath him. The edges of the afternoon have started to disintegrate; the foggy sunlight giving way to grainy dusk. Jasper's ears prick up suddenly – a new sound – footsteps, human footsteps, he can tell by their heavy clumsiness. And voices, a man and a woman's.... the familiar, soothing voices of home.

Jasper opens his mouth to bark.

"Listen!" Jasmine stops dead, clutching Harry's arm. They both pause, heads cocked to one side.

"There it is again!" she says, "Did you hear it Harry? A bark?"

Harry turns to face Jasmine, a hesitant smile spreading across his face. Then it comes again, clearer this time – a definite bark. Harry nods wildly, pointing to the left. "It's coming from over there," he says grabbing Jasmine's hand, "Come on – Jasper!" he calls, as they both run along the muddy path.

"Jasper!" they both shout in unison, their voices echoing in the advancing darkness of the woods.

There is silence for a moment before the little dog comes bursting out of the undergrowth, wet and shaking with cold, but his little tail wagging insanely as they both kneel to scoop him up. They are both laughing with relief, hugging and stroking down Jasper's wet fur. In their excitement Jasmine lets Harry pull her towards him, kiss the top of her head. The three of them bunch together in an awkward cuddle as Harry takes off his jacket to wrap up the shivering dog.

"He looks like he did that day I saw him at the shelter," says Harry, as their laughter dies down. "So small and vulnerable..."

Jasmine strokes Jasper's ears as Harry wraps him tightly. She puts her face close to the dog's.

"Do you forgive us for arguing?" she asks him. Jasper licks her hand.

"Come on," says Harry, "Let's go home."

But Jasmine doesn't move right away, her face is frozen in thought.

"He belongs to us, doesn't he," she says softly.

"You mean Jasper?" Harry asks.

"I can't imagine him not being here, with us." Jasmine looks up at Harry uncertainly. "It's worked out okay hasn't it, adopting Jasper? I mean apart from today," she tucks a strand of hair behind her ear.

"Do you think maybe we *could* do that for a child, Harry?"

"What?" he asks, confused. Then, as understanding dawns, a slow, incredulous smile spreads across his face. "You mean adopt?"

Jasmine nods, returning his smile.

"I mean, we've got a lot to fix Harry, a lot, and I'm not promising anything..." she says, but Harry sees a new light of possibility in her hazel eyes; the faintest glint of hope.

"Come on," he whispers, motioning to Jasper, who is still shaking in her arms. "Let's get him home and we can talk things through."

"Man is the only animal for whom his own existence
is a problem which he has to solve."

Erich Fromm – German born American social philosopher
and psychoanalyst, 1900 - 1980

THE PAGEANT
Angela Songui

The Designer is pacing, stopping only to peek through the curtains at the ballroom filling with a tide of smug and glamour: the judges taking their seats, the photographers vying for choicest position at the end of the catwalk, the bulging throng that flatten their wide bottoms on the cushions of spindly gilt chairs. In this moment of surveillance, Owen clutches his rolling stomach and holds fast to the curtain lip; his typical pre-show jitters leave a sweaty residue that crushes the red velvet drapery into a grapey pulp in his damp palm.

Backstage, the security doors part with violent thunder and metallic alarm, a burst of cheapening daylight floods the cavernous hall holding for a moment in freeze frame the outlines of the bustle within: squinting eyes, mouths arrested in "O's" of surprise, clapping hands, snapping fingers; sashes, flowers, programmes flapping and fanning as assistants run back and forth with hairbrushes, garment bags and bottles of expensive imported waters.

Naomii's guardian stands in repulsive silhouette against the glare of outdoors, in a vintage fur stole and black too-tight cat suit, a lumpy shadow from a child's nightmares. With a jangle of charms, the only in her possession, she prods her young charge forward offering her up to the room and relinquishes her claim with a grandiose proclamation of leaving 'her baby in capable hands', smearing lipstick skid marks in her pursuit of the best seat in the house. Slamming shut, the heavy doors cut off the outside world of churlish delivery vans, blaring car-horns and careening rubbish bin lids; the dressing hall activity resumes unabated and Owen swoops down upon his Muse, all flailing hands and puckering lips,

- Finally! Where have you been? Never mind...you're here.

Terrance – get Naomii into the chair; Number 1 – get the dress. No, not that one, the red one, the red one. How did you get this job again? We have fifteen minutes 'til Opening Promenade, people, then Holidays on Parade – look ALIVE!
Terrance unfurls an arsenal of brushes and combs,

- Look at that hair... What have you been up to all night, Miss Congeniality?

Naomii sighs and closes her lids allowing hands both strange and familiar to prepare her for the day ahead, while reflecting on the pawing she enjoyed just the night before.

*****

The sweater is too tight, of course.
It strangles in new and unusual ways - too tight at the wrists and an hourglass cinch in the waistline that manages to be both bindingly curvaceous and unflattering. The Designer, planting sloppy two-cheek kisses on anyone passing, traces dervish circles into the carpet, pausing every few seconds to nervously fuss with the collar even though the photo-shoot portion of the proceedings has been over for about ten minutes already. The photographer has discreetly slipped his equipment back into their neat black cases and himself out of Owen Tweely's line of vision. Owen, conspicuous in one of his own creations, meanwhile, is on a rampage about the next pageant segment and the lousy quality of bottled water available backstage. Finger crooked down the neck of her sweater Owen gently tugs Naomii's face towards his own, purring into her ear,

> - Swiss water! I specifically wanted *Swiss* water. Doesn't anyone deliver my requirements notes anymore? Well, at least the wine is French. How do they work like this, these people?

He nuzzles at her with his nose and though she appears to smile Naomii's neck muscles involuntarily convulse and pull her head back ever so slightly. With the Ball Gown segment coming up in twenty minutes there's enough time for additional re-touches to hair and makeup, another brushing, another teasing, another dab of Vaseline on the teeth.

At least she'll be out of this damned 'Snuggly Seasonal' cat's-cradle straightjacket. Naomii allows herself to be led to her private room in the dressing area, away from the stations set up for the other contestants, more gentle hands stroking her back, assuring her that the worst is possibly over. That is until the epic struggle of removing the sweater begins. It takes both assistants to get the contraption up and over her head yet it lodges stubbornly for a few panicky seconds behind her ears. Uncomfortable silence is swiftly filled with a pantomime torrent of exclamations: throaty cries of pain from Naomii, the assistants feigning surprise and dismay, and near-death-experience from Owen who surges into the room with the force of an electric current. In that second she can only hear the clink of bottles and jars being jostled on her vanity, the snickering Assistants, furiously busy footfalls and the *schink-schtuck* of metal legs snapping into place on the massage table, all against the ebb and flow from the greater dressing hall activity. The up-close rushing of woollen tides tug and stroke her delicate lobes stuffing them momentarily with balls of yarn. Assistant Number 1 sports a wounded hand from having accidentally tugged too sharply on Naomii's tresses before Promenade and absently presses the Band-Aid to her lips holding back tears. Naomii shakes her mane free with a hint of indifference; a hiss of disapproval escapes from The Designer's coin-purse lips,

- An Owen Tweely Tog must be treated with *respect*.
Lurking ominously against the back of the door, now swung shut in Owen's wake, a beige garment bag swishes hypnotically from side to side – all eyes focus then fall from the gilt 'OTT' tattooed across its chest as Assistant Number 1.5 (she refuses to be known as Number 2) deftly arrests the sway with fingers practiced in subtle correction.

Naomii has been Owen's Muse for two years now, a job she sometimes enjoys, taking not-so-secret pleasure in her tantrums and outbursts for which she is renowned and yet rapidly forgiven. Normally she is cool and unruffled but on occasion she blows long and hot, like a Santa Anna, in any random direction especially after spending an hour trussed up like a Christmas turkey in knitted seasonal bondage wear. A breeze creeps in from the open window high in the wall of her dressing room and cuts a gently rolling path through the powder, hairspray and scented colognes to the tip of her nose, pauses, then teases her to sniff at its strangeness: the allure of food smells, car exhaust, the breath of indistinguishable conversations passing by, cigarettes, wet pavement, the approach of evening, of nightfall.

The masseur, glowing white next to his table, gently pats its padded top after laying a fresh towel down for her to stretch out upon. There's always time for a rubdown, her favourite part of the

whole stupid day. Under the shoulder blades roughly, up along her
neck then down her spine, repeated with confidence and precision,
        - Oooo, you're so tense, child...

        More relaxed now, and into the makeup chair: brushing,
blowing, curling, teasing, hands fly all about her; the temptation
to strike them is great but manageable. Waxy bristles flatten the
sounds of fawning and cooing in the room. In the mirror there is
a flourish of ingenuous servitude and ingratiating smiles. Owen
flapping about, a great flightless bird crowing instructions and
splashing the floor with his champagne, as Numbers 1 and 1.5 set
the pendulum of OTT's bland trappings in motion, slapping at
each other's fingers to be the one who pulls the zipper, the one who
reveals the contents to the ooo-ing and ahhhh-ing entourage. A look
of utter contempt flashes like a blade, quickly sheathed in a bath of
accolade and the search for an imagined stray thread on his jacket;
Owen tries on some 'humble genius' in the mirror and turns to face
the room. Then with a swish of his wrists the suit bag settles and
with a yawn spills forth a churning froth of crinoline and tulle over
his shoes. Naomii closes her eyes and surrenders to the inevitable.
        - Yes, mint and sea foam; My Vision – The Mermaids of the
        Sea!
        - But mint isn't an aquatic...
Through wilting gauze, Number 1 sucks at the wound on the back of
her hand and eyes Owen with masochistic admiration, while 1.5 tries
to slink her way out of the ice-pick glare of Owen's spotlight.
        - Ballgown, people – Let's DO IT...

        A flock of expert hands take flight and in a flurry of strap-
ping, unhooking, zipping and fluffing the bodice of the gown is in
place – another improbable waistline that pushes her bum high
in the air. The sequins and pailettes create a dance of light that
distracts for a moment or two, then expanding the sides of her
constricted ribcage to their fullest, Naomii inhales as deeply as is
possible and releases her very best 'don't pay so much attention to
ME' moan.
        From behind hooded lids she watches Owen - knee-high in
undulations of pale green, turn and armed with a mouthful of safety
pins - attach the train, or rather tail, to the back of the bodice. Every
hair now in place, an irresistible far-away stare fixed in her gaze, all
eyes drink her up and down. As if by tidal momentum, Naomii is

heaved up the stairs and nosed through the heavy velvet drapery with Owen still gathering armfuls of sea foam trailing behind.

Gelled and coloured lights, artificial fog, and one-two-three-four paces; the tail of the gown continues to pour from between the still-parted lips of curtain framing Owen, The Designer: proudly expectant, gleaming with apprehension and avarice, stepping forward in his immaculate shoes, silver buckles polished to a supernova flare. Flash of light and forward motion for both walkers, one trailing the sea and the other catching a wave; Owen's starlit foot comes to rest on a scalloped edge of veil, his buckle casting a frantic searchlight across the faces of those seated in the dim. With dilated pupils Naomii follows the tiny comet tail which streaks across rapacious expressions, then the ceiling, then down the far wall of the ballroom to the end of the catwalk where it jigs a teasing burlesque. Strobing cameras make a blurred tunnel of the catwalk and she continues with in-born stealth and purpose towards the pin-prick of light dancing up ahead. Then – SNAP – like a wave coming to shore with a jerk and a slap and a great ragged sound, Naomii is pulled taught to a temporary stop, then thrust forward. The ghastly ripping noises behind her sound an alarm that begins as a low mournful howling and grows to a full-fledged shrill of despair so contagious that it breeds a viral hysteria throughout the ballroom. Owen lunges awkwardly through the velvet slash, a bawling infant clutching at tatters of his creation in vain attempt to contain the seascape of satin and tulle, both his feet take turns at staking Naomii's Mermaid's tail firmly to the floor.

Shaking her head from side to side to rid her ears of Owen's siren, Naomii's tiara soars, a sparkling boomerang, as it detaches from her head and lands with a great sploink in the water pitcher on the Judges Table causing all four adjudicators to leap backwards to avoid the splashes and send their chairs crashing into the knees of the greedy pageant cling-on's behind them. More shrieks and more shouting, more flashbulbs flashing and shutters clicking, adjustments to outfits and the wiping of imaginary stains; the room is caught in a tableau of overreaction and exaggerated gesture. Naomii, freed from her Mermaid's tail, seizes her chance and with an almost prescient grace, she surfs the tide of panic now flooding the room out through the service doors, coasting behind a waiter and his tray load of tuna sashimi. Although bedecked in spangle and sequin, Naomii is near-invisible amidst the hustle of waitstaff and moves herself easily between each shifting skidding tray and trolley in the service corridor towards the EXIT. Slipping like a shadow into the promise of cooling air in the alleyway outside, she pauses for a moment and rests against the rough brick wall, enjoying the brush of its grit on her cheek and the sweet perfume of rotting garbage rising from the bins and asphalt.

    - I knew you'd come...

    - I knew you'd be waiting

He sits there on the lip of the low wall opposite, and though seated manages to swagger, one leg dangling lazily. Glowing golden in the final rays of the afternoon he smoothly descends to the ground like a sunset. Her Lover, whose dancing eyes play with mischievous purpose in his otherwise inscrutable face. Now laughing at the sight of her bustled like a transvestite pigeon in the shreds of Owen's finery, he quickly succumbs to her silent plea for assistance to be free of these ludicrous trappings of glamour. They reunite in a furious passion, each pulling, tugging, tearing tooth and nail at corset, strap and binding until nothing remains but themselves, the night-softened sounds of the city and the gathering dark. The last strips of cloth and feather fall away – unashamed in her nakedness and shining black in the sodium lamplight, Naomii shakes her magnificent coat in the evening breezes and turns her shining eyes on her Lover. She purrs an endearment and runs.

Runs into the night, runs for her life...all nine of them.

"The kind man feeds his beast before sitting down to dinner."

Hebrew Proverb

RAT LOVE
Amarpreet Basi

*

Underneath the staircase is a cage of rats. Boris is the daddy and he is blind. Mrs Gregory is the matriarch and Longpeach, Diamond and Lightning are the children. They spend their lives worming and wriggling through the little houses and sliding tubes Marylyn has arranged for them. One of these houses is a suspended sphere with a circular opening in its centre. To reach it, the rats have to race to the top tier of the cage and jump the distance. When they aren't interested in their little city of adventure, they scramble up the walls of the cage, their twitching noses poking out of the tiny squares in the grid. I don't know what they're thinking when they do this; maybe they want to be free.

These are Marylyn's rats and she loves them.

*

Marylyn and I had returned to the house after an evening out. After slinging her handbag and coat over the banister, she crouched before the cage.

– Did you miss Mommy? Do you want to come out and give me a kiss?

I was jealous. She never spoke to me like that.

The cage door dropped open and Boris scampered up her right arm, over her neck and back down her other arm. Marylyn laughed at the tickles Boris's little paws made. She turned to me and suggested Boris should say hello. Before I could demur, it was already on me, tunnelling through my jumper and up to my shoulder. I became hysterical and pleaded with her to remove it from me but she was beside herself with laughter. Now Boris was between my shoulder blades, venturing downwards. I pulled my jumper over me and he came somersaulting out. He landed on his feet and then, as if by instinct, found his way back inside the cage. By this time Marylyn was in hysterics. She was hugging her stomach and convulsing with laughter. I was happy she was happy but just to be sure another rat didn't use me as a climbing frame, I flipped the cage door shut with the toe of my shoe. I lifted Marylyn to her feet and guided her to the kitchen. Before I had crossed the threshold, my foot hit the cage and the metal rang out. She whirled around and glared at me.

– What do you think you are doing?

– What? I just accidentally hit the cage with my foot. What's the problem?

– To you that sound wasn't loud but to their little ears it's like a really big earthquake. Keep that in mind next time.

Next time what? Next time I accidentally nudge the cage? What kind of logic was that? By the time I had sucked in some air to rebut her she had already turned her back on me and was heading towards the sink.

– Would you like a cup of tea? She was filling the kettle with a burst of water.

I said I would and sat there at the table thinking about the rats. I wanted some of that rat-love from her. I thought of my own mother, and the excitement of seeing her blurred orange salwar kameez approaching the frosted glass of her front door.

Marylyn turned on her CD player and a Hendrix song came on. She began to dance. It was a slow, swaying dance and her eyes were closed. She sang out the lyrics, sometimes loudly and at other times she whispered them. She stopped when the kettle reached the boil. She poured the tea and asked me if I liked Hendrix's music. I mumbled an answer about how I appreciated the cultural signifi-cance of his music and how I really wanted to like it but unfortu-nately couldn't because I couldn't get past the scratchiness of the guitar. She frowned at this answer. I was disappointed that I had dis-appointed her. She set the tea before me and sat down. Her posture was impeccable. I corrected mine.

– Well, look, you've really got to brush up on your musical awareness. It's like really bad. I mean you don't know Hendrix, Mar-ley, Weller. You're into that really ghetto stuff. Oh my God, it's so crass and unbecoming, you know? If you want to be middle-class and not just another Asian from Birmingham, you've got to start educating yourself. Listen to Bach, Barber, listen to something with intellectuality.

She wasn't middle-class herself, but she wanted to be.

– But I don't want to be middle-class. I don't want to be any class! You keep talking about class, I don't understand why it means so much to you. Different people are different, that's all.

My phone rang. It was my brother, Aman.

– Yo, what's crackulating, baby? Son, I got that new Rae-kwon and Enrique Inglasias joint on smash! That's on heavy rotatio–

– I'm with someone. Can I call you back please?

– Please? Why you talking like a white boy for? Who you with, some birds?

– Yeah.

– Social life!

– Something like that.

– '*I got sexy ladies, ooh-ooooh, all over the floor!*' But yo, is it with Crazy Woman?

– Yeah. Look: I'll call you back.

– Son, I got three words for you: Blood. Pressure. Machine. Anyone that gets off on medical equi–

I hung up. Seconds later he texted back: *oi, hanging up on me? Judas. I'm telling mum.* I apologised to Marylyn and said it was someone from work with a question about our QA servers.

We stopped talking. Nina Simone's *Wild Is The Wind* was playing. I was galvanised by its melancholy. I could ride its chords into her dark mind. I slid my hand along the table. She eyed it with suspicion. When our hands made contact she quickly retreated hers.

– What are you playing at?

– I'm sorry. I was just thinking about you and Boris. How you liked to hug him and play with him.

– So?

– I wish you would like to hug and play with me sometimes.

– For God's sake! He's a rat! Yeah OK then, I'll hug you and cuddle you. What else would you like? Should I also put you in a big nappy, breastfeed you and rock you to sleep? Would you like that?

– No, of course not. Well, maybe the breastfeeding bit but you know what I mean. Contact. That's what I want. Just to touch you once in a while.

– Well, I told you before, I don't do kisses, I don't do

touching. If that's what you're looking for, go out and find it.

Living with my flatmate wasn't easy. She once told me, long ago, that she was "incapable of love". I wouldn't have persisted had there not been certain wordless moments I continually mistook for attraction. She rejected me all the time. And whenever she did, my own weaknesses would surface: if I could not have a partner's love, I would implore her for a mother's love.

– Is it because you don't trust me? What is it? You're so opaque, I don't understand how your mind works. You should, you know, let me in, let me help you or whatever. Let's talk about it. Or something.

She cackled.

– Look at you trying to be some kind of therapist! Giving me a pep talk. Look, I told you, I'm just not interested.

I made a final attempt to persuade her, this time with a bottom-of-the-barrel-scraped metaphor that didn't even convince me.

– We're all rats in this city, Marylyn. We're all scurrying around, knocking into one another, living these looped lives. I think what you did to Boris there was wonderful. Holding him like that every once in a while gives him sustenance. I think if we could do that for one another, that would give us, I don't know, some kind of spiritual nourishment or something.

She laughed hard.

– Bollocks. You're just mad you can't sleep with me.

I gave up. For the remainder of the evening I sat quiet and nodded to every beat of Marylyn's tutelage on Good Music. It somehow became a spoken essay on race and class, on the British black experience of the 60s and 70s, on the mod sub-culture, on old 45rpm reggae records, on the schisms between the alleged altruisms of socialism and the inarguable callousness of Thatcherism, on riots and unions, on taxes and cuts, on colonialism and the alienation of mulatto people (herself included) and many other topics. I didn't know enough about these things and I suspected she didn't either. Every now and then I tried to ask an innocent question and I was rebuked because, apparently, the question revealed my gross ignorance. I was trying to argue that we were free-thinking beings that could do whatever we wanted to do and be whatever we wanted to be. But that notion angered her. Though she never put it like this, I think the subtext of her speech was that some people were on the bottom and some were at the top, and she was angered by the lines that demarcated these sets, blaming it all on some grand hegemony that she wanted to become a part of. She fetishised it. She was confusing.

The soundtrack continued in the background. By the time we had reached Kasabian's Fire, she was too caught up in its chorus to bother telling me anything else. I watched her dance in the glow of the dim bulb-light. She looked, at that particular moment, completely free. I quietly rose to my feet and headed off upstairs. I stopped by the cage to look at the rats one last time. Just as I rounded the corner to the foot of the stairs, she called after me.

– What?

– Come here.

I went back to the kitchen. What new humiliation was this?

She held out her arms. I looked her in the eye to check she wasn't joking. I stepped into her hug and put my arms around her. I lost myself in the nook of her neck and shoulder, burying myself into the fuzzy black wool of her cardigan. My ear folded against her neck and the curls of her kinky hair tickled my forehead. I want to report how wonderful this moment was but the truth is, after the frisson of her skin brushing mine, it became become stiff and she became distant. It was as if she offered the gesture out of a pity that was decided upon, but not emotionally borne. Or perhaps it was genuine and just short-lived. I squeezed tighter, assuring myself that contrived intimacy was better than nothing. I waited for her to admonish me and free herself with a brusque shove to my chest. The embrace had turned awkward and a crick had crept its way into my neck.

– Go on, that's enough now. Don't milk it…

"Horse sense is the thing a horse has which keeps it from betting on people."

W. C. Fields – comedian, actor, writer, 1880 - 1946

BOUNCING SILHOUETTES
Josephine Dexter

*

It was impossible for Joy to continue in her high-heeled sandals. She was clearly limping as she quickened to catch him up.

"You hurt?" asked Tate.

She shook her head. His coat, heavy on her shoulders, had trapped her long bright hair. They were both still shaken. The others had left in different directions; the car was a wreck, so everybody was walking back. Tate was annoyed he'd taken the last lift home from the May dance. Now it was gone two in the morning and he was stuck on a lonely road with a girl who insisted they'd see oncoming headlights soon. Tate didn't know Joy that well, she was a few years younger than him, but she lived and worked in his village so he was charged with getting her home.

He propped himself against a field gate. The distant village was camouflaged with night; everyone in Nettlesby turned their lights out after midnight. Just like the bloody war, thought Tate. He pointed it out for her.

"I know where I am," she said.

"Only trouble is, fastest way back's right here, through the pastures." He hoisted himself from the gate, fully expecting her to favour the road with its possibility of rescue. She continued to stare out at the valley, barely visible past the dense, inky patches of trees and the dampness rising like fine threads of mould.

"But I must get back fast. Before first light," she tilted her face towards the modest moon. "See how it's in its last quarter? Well, he's not so pretty, my father, 'round this time."

So the fields it was. Joy unfastened her shoes and flexed her slender

31

feet. Tate hastily proffered his shoes, like two ripe specimens of fruit, but they were ridiculously oversized and she resigned to a journey barefoot. He then perplexed her with some ungainly frog-hopping and, genuflecting before her, he doubled his long socks over her feet.

The chill ground was a shock to her. She resisted his supporting arm to begin with but was soon whimpering: "Oh Tate, do slow down. I'm sure I shall tread on something horrid."

Tate checked his pace; his athletic legs had taken off on their own account.

"Don't you worry lass," he said as she caught up. "I work on this land...know every thistle. There's nowt here to mind."

"What a talent! Knowing where every sheep has emptied itself." Patting down her bottle-blonde waves, freed at last from the coat collar, she squinted with doubt over the murky ground. The kingfisher-blue chiffon that had helped to shower her with advances at the dance was now poking out from the bottom of his coat, bunched and colourless. Even those fearsomely scarlet lips were black against the moon.

"Can you see that bright spot just below?"
She didn't answer.

"That's the river. If we get down level with it, the light'll stay with us all the way home." And with that he clicked his tongue and winked. This was a mistake. She averted her eyes with a disgust that tore at his insides. Again, he tried to take her arm, but she protested with a shrug. So he moved on.

"Are y' coming?" he eventually shouted, not turning.

She silently reached him; he kept his back to her, watching the river; listening to its intricate tinkling.

"How's the socks?" he finally said, pushing off.

"Ralf and Bailey are saying your family are selfish, not to let the shooters in," she said.

They were two of the lads they'd been travelling back with. She'd spent most of the night with them. Tate didn't like them much. So full of their War Service anecdotes of trials and deprivations – it pained him immensely.

"Farmer Smyke takes his share the rest of the year," he said, bristling at the turn of conversation. "What twaddle! The rooks are good for the crop, eating grubs and such like..."

"I've heard it before too. The village says that in wartime

32

they would have fed some families – the young ones, not yet flown. They're the ones you eat."

"You forget. One year we let them in. The next our family tragedy... My ma's funny 'bout it. Reckons there was summit in it."

She paused, catching his meaning, and they left the river for a time to cross a small wood.

They walked sightlessly beneath the ceiling of leaves, through which filtered occasional lunar ghosts. The scent of sleeping wood anemones and bluebells mixed in with Joy's perfumed earlobes as she drew close to him, appreciative now of his guiding arm around her shoulders.

"I used to be scared of your house. I thought the trees were haunted by spirits of the dead."

"It's just a rookery," he laughed.

Something stirred in the undergrowth nearby, and the loud alarm-call of a pheasant shot outwards, echoing against the trees further back. Shocked, she grabbed him, "But aren't you frightened? It's so isolated up there."

"I don't know it any other way."

The path was wet and muddy in places, creating surprises in the dark, "I feel I might be stepping on a corpse," she said.

Tate froze for a second and she swiped his back, "I'm being silly."

No, he thought. Not so foolish to imagine treading on the dead.

By the river light, they rested against a fallen tree and he removed a sticky bud, with difficulty, from her hair. She was getting tired; her head lolled towards him when he tugged it.

"Do you think you'll stay here? Forever, I mean," she said.

"What else is there? Here's good as anywhere."

She sunk into herself.

"And you?"

"I'm saving, see, to move into Mulberton. Reckon I'll find a husband there."

"You do?"

Heavy now, her eyebrows mustered a twitch, "Nobody ever comes here. Nothing and nobody."

He saw her to the door. It was sad helping her out of his

coat. Those delicate arms like the limbs of a fawn were so vulnerable and her muddied legs and stubbed toes needed attention. He returned her heels and she peeled off the sodden socks, making a joke about it being oh-so romantic. Then she smiled up at him, her face moving in, lips stretching drowsily over her tiny, overlapping teeth. They were pearls that reappeared in the muted light as he hugged his warm coat about him on the climb home.

**

"Read that aggin for Tate." His father stretched an arthritic finger, weakened by amusement, towards the back dresser. They were sitting round a tea of bread, butter and pilchards. His mother lifted the letter in her greasy fingers.

"Can you guess who?" she spat cryptically, over the table-cloth. Tate stirred his tea.

She began to read, *"Dear Aunt Edina and Uncle Sidney–"*
"Cousin Will, o' course!"

"I have a business proposition to make to you. I have great visions of this country moving out of the shadows. There is going to be a change in what we decide to sit on and whoever taps into this will be sitting on a fortune. It is now au-spicious to start–"

"Talks grand, this fellow."

"Ssshh Sidney...*to start my own shop. I have found a lovely building in Nottingham, but need a second party to come in on the investment side. This is where I enquire about your interest,"* she wiped her eyes with the corner of her apron, *"seventy pounds should be sufficient at this minute and I would welcome you as partners with a percentage share..."*

Tate jumped at the force behind the old man's laugh. Abandoning the tea, he shook his head and grinned broadly as the cutlery rattled with mirth.

"You better watch it Sid," his mother shrieked. "He's after your gold bullions." This provoked a second round of howling. We are noisier than the birds, thought Tate.

"What was that?" His mother's large, blotchy face shot up. Tate, the most astute, was sure it was a car door. They weren't expecting anyone.

Hearing a crunch of feet outside, Tate checked his appearance in the front-door mirror. The October light was fading. In the shadows he could've been a teenager; his head reminded him of the turnip speared on a broom pole that Smyke had got him to erect in one of the fields. Stroking his oiled-back hair, he paused. The advancing footsteps had ceased. There was the usual clamour of corvine sociability from the trees opposite, nothing else. As he concentrated on the sounds, a mature Tate, suited and imperative, caught his eye in the mirror. But it wasn't a reflection of him at all: it was Will. There was nobody suited and imperative in Nettlesby.

Opening the door on the emerging twilight, the footsteps resumed like the trudging of a pulse. He stepped out, and again it hushed. The house was a severe limestone fortification; its raised doorway had a narrow porch, accessed from the yard by stone steps. Tate remained within the porch's confines, spotting Smyke's truck parked at a steep incline beyond the yard. The thought of Smyke watching at some vantage point unknown was unsettling, but then came the realization that he was just below on the other side of the porch, back against the wall in the cobweb gloom. So Tate waited, and with every breath he heard a deeper breathing overlaying his. The breathing brought about the carnality of the man, the moist upper lip, the blown-out eye; only the warmth eluded Tate. His chest began to rise and fall in time with it; the unspeakable terror catching in his lungs. Just then a dark shape scurried behind the rookery trees not two hundred yards away. It was Smyke, hell-bent in the direction of his truck.

"Hey," cried Tate. But it was futile.

For a moment, Tate believed that two men had paid him a visit. But as Smyke drove off, the mysterious breathing subsided and there were no more footsteps. He chuckled with relief. Smyke had never loitered in the rookery before. But Smyke wasn't all there, everyone knew that. Tate sprung down the steps and took a circuit of the property; just to be sure he was alone. The farmer was a solitary individual, with no wife. He was never right after what happened, years back. They said he was left hanging upside down all night. When they found him he was still conscious, but without sight – bawling, he was, like those burnt badly in the war. They never found who constructed that crude trap on Smyke senior's private land. Poachers, most likely. Smyke senior, normally such a gentle man, put up a cash reward for a name, and promised to do unmentionable things to the culprit. He went to his grave not knowing. Words came back to Smyke within a couple of weeks but they didn't follow the same patterns as before. His thinking was slow, and then came in bursts of impulsive incoherence. Although one side recovered, his right eye, which had popped like a light bulb, was deadened.

Tate was striding over the grass that fringed the front of the house when he saw it. A long-handled axe had been plunged into the ground. Pinned to the earth by this action was a crude piece of cardboard with words scrawled in sheep dip. With some force, Tate released the blade to read:

> *Last chanse squib!*
> *If the rooks dunt go then the trees do*
> *see to it*
> *or else be dun with yer and niver come work back for me*
> *aggin.*

The footfall had been real at least.

The next day he was sent home from work. Smyke's appointed spokesperson, Valliers, came rushing out of the stable block. "What you done?" he shouted.

Tate, unable to answer, shrugged his canvas bag up his shoulder and continued over the cobblestones. The man jounced him from behind,

"Smyke says he gives you a week to fix it. You're not to come back till it's done."

Tutting's Farm had employed Tate since he was a gawky fourteen-year-old, nine years past. It had been a lot different back then when the old man, Smyke senior, was in charge. He had an affectionate way of working with nature; as he set Tate to his tasks, picking up stones or sending him off with a large rake into the fields, he delighted in the elucidation of a particular wagtail, flicking it's tail in the dusty yard entrance; or the identification of certain tall grasses that he tore back with his stick. It had no bearing on Tate's life really, knowing the name of a Pearl Bordered Fritillary, but he was glad of the enrichment of his otherwise mundane jobs. When, six years ago, Smyke senior passed away, his son took on the farm. Things changed. Absent more often than not, he was found conducting himself mindlessly about the local town. Whilst his father had worn the stains of the soil on his hands, Smyke's looked a little cleaner, but he was otherwise unshaven, and smelt none too pleasant. The village was patient, and waited for the grieving process to abate. But, after several months, important decisions were failing to be made, and it seemed pretty clear that the new farmer was shirking, they said, from his responsibilities.

Suddenly one day Smyke emerged fuelled with an aggression never seen before. Within a year he had torn up many of the ancient hedgerows dividing the fields to maximize the yield and grant easier access for his new machinery. Creatures were marooned as they crossed these vast, barren fields and became easy prey for Smyke's shotgun which he had taken to walking about with. Gradually he became obsessed with the corvids: the most fearless of pests. The rooks in particular had an elusive cunning; they attacked his seedlings and feasted on his wheat and were the greatest aggravation. He needed to get to them early, before they developed their shyness of guns; when they were still awkward on the branches. But he never could because the rookery, deemed centuries-old, with over forty nests, notwithstanding a colony of jackdaws – the nucleus of corvine life – stood within the boundaries of Tate's house.

***

Tate was far above the ladder when he got his first pang of dread; a dizziness that made the leafy ground spin, way below the boughs of the tree. And in a sudden breezy upsurge, the larger branches were rocking him about. He'd climbed fearlessly until now, the saw strapped to his back, the ends of his trousers tucked into his rough socks, shaking off the uneasy draught that came at his chest through his shirt. Anger and misery had spurred him upwards. Soon it would all be destroyed, and for what? Just so life could continue as dully and as comfortlessly as before?

The student hired hands had all left now that summer had ended. He knew she had been interested in one of them: a fair-headed geography undergraduate called Lucas. Tate had worked with him, weeding the kale. He took his time – always resting his back when he reached the end of a line. Tate had longed for Joy to see them working alongside one another; then she'd see who the real man was: Tate could work down the fields like a machine. But he only saw her a few times in the evening, after her shift at the shop; her arms crossed over a gate, talking to Lucas. The night of the dance was seemingly all but forgotten; to everyone, that was, except

Tate.

The leaves, much denser up here, were filtering the sun-light, giving Tate the impression he was in a sort of ethereal lamp-light. He might have fallen already, such was his light-headedness; he didn't feel real anymore. He had started to pick out individual voices in the general cawing, and, once or twice, a toppling of small twigs and musty debris fell onto his upturned face. Perhaps that, or the altitude, had caused his eyes to smart and water. He had become rigid suddenly, hugging the thick branch he'd been scaling. With his ear to the bark, he could hear the steady creaking of the tree, the peaceful susurration of the foliage corresponding with the gentle inflections of light; the noisy rookery becoming a background blur against these subtleties.

The vale gradually came into focus through a gap in the branches and he saw an elevated and partial view of the village, like an unfinished jigsaw puzzle, dusty in the distance. He couldn't look upon the village without thoughts of Joy, going about her business somewhere below those rooftops. Probably on her shift, stamping the ration books with that red ink that reminded him so much of the rouged kiss she planted on his lips that night he got her home safely. The wave of grief that consumed him at the thought dragged him out of his paralysis. Once again he dug into the bark and clawed himself towards the darting and bouncing silhouettes above.

He was suddenly aware that they could easily mob him now that he was upon the nests. Thankfully all the chicks had fledged, but he was still an impostor, woefully vulnerable in their high canopy. Most had risen from the tree, their cries of alarm – ARRGH ARRGH ARRGH! – tearing the air, as they circled in an intimidating formation above the stand of trees, racing with the occupants of the nests further along. Tate peered into the bulky construction of twigs and was surprised at the scent of old feathers matted with dried faeces and moss – as pungent as someone's house. He identified the foundations of the nest and started to untie the saw. Only one rook appeared to challenge him directly. He perched, guardedly, a couple of feet from the nest; he was large and aged, his cere especially bald. Tate pressed his knees into the branch, angling the saw-blade; its teeth biting the bark like a succulent apple. The rook lowered his beak, tail in the air, and lunged forward with cries of outrage. He did this several times, but kept a marked distance from Tate. He knows, thought Tate, suddenly slipping forward as the wind skewed his positioning. And then he saw it. Just inside the rim of the nest. It twinkled like a falling water droplet caught in the sun. Tate hoped it wasn't a shower starting. As he repositioned himself, the leaves shuddered in an updraft and there came a series of twinkles, like angelic notes. The branches heaved like a ship's prow, and a further set of sparkling winks made him wary of some other creature in the nest. His tough, brown fingers investigated, feeling nothing at first, and he suspected it nothing more than an iridescent snail trail that had dried against the sticks; the nest was fairly creeping with bugs after all. But his finger and thumb suddenly closed in on something as hard as a ball bearing, and, as his thumb pressed in further, he felt a linkage. He pulled it carefully, disentangling it from the mesh of twigs; it swung from his fingers, as pendulous as a train of saliva. Resting just inside the crook of his hand, attached to the intricate chain, was a diamond: a solitary, multi-faceted pear-drop. The saw plummeted to the ground.

Tate didn't tell anyone why he'd gone into Leicester instead of Mulberton. When he'd cleaned the necklace it blazed with superiority; he'd never seen anything quite so stunning in his life. His first instinct was to give it to Joy. She was the only person he knew glamorous enough to wear it. She certainly had the outfits. But something stopped him. What if it was of significant value?

So he approached an out-of-town jeweller, anticipating questions – he didn't look like the type, with his coarse brown suit and wrong type of hat, to be carrying such wealth.

A dark-suited and imperative gentleman was keen to give it careful examination. So intrigued was he that he asked permission to call in a colleague from a neighbouring establishment. There was a lot of head scratching and the inevitable questions that Tate was dreading. Where had it come from? How long had his family owned it? Tate said that it had been with the family for as long as he knew, that he thought a particular ancestor working at a big house had received it on retirement. "It's not especially old," the second gentleman intervened. The necklace sat between them, mounted royally on dark-blue velvet. "And what was the value given at the time of receipt?" chimed the other. Tate said he really wasn't sure. All he knew was that it was an heirloom they were now being forced to sell, having met with such poverty since his brother had died in the war. This last bit was true at least, and both men eased off, swallowing respectfully. "I would be glad to make a purchase," the first gentleman assured.

"Can you do it today?" asked Tate.

Out in the frisky midday light, Tate stumbled along the pavement, giddy, as if he'd been punched. He finally came to rest against the windowsill of a public house. Pedestrians shuttled past him, the blustery wind meddling with their coats. He needed a drink to sober up. Entering that dim den of pipe-smoke, he was suddenly wary, and when he left the bar he sat bolt upright against the balding wallpaper, anxious not to stand out as a target for swindlers. A sip of gin refreshed his mouth. If he chose judiciously he could have a car and more. He'd be able to give Joy the freedom to go anywhere she wished. He could drive her to see every picture in town, and they could attend all the dances. Tate's mind raced. How did a person go about buying a car anyway? While he pondered this he strode into a tailor's and chose a sleek suit, off-the-peg. A hat would have been nice, but somehow he didn't have the nerve. The car would arouse enough speculation in due course.

He returned as he came, on the Mulberton bus, stopping briefly in Mulberton to buy a bouquet of miniature roses. The Post Office's entrance bell sounded celestial. Glad of just a couple of children, ogling jars of aniseed balls and Catherine Wheels, he waited for Joy to serve them, flowers pressed behind his back. She resumed leaning on her elbows over an open magazine on the counter, something of which she was always in good supply. When he spoke her eyes flashed up at him and she answered with a thin, self-conscious smile; she had a habit of movie-star posturing. He paused for a moment, letting her take in his handsome attire,

"Can I meet with you, after work?"

She snatched a glance towards the doorway behind the counter.

"It's just...I've something to tell you. Fantastic news."

She seemed apprehensive. Her father, he thought, was in the vicinity. He was postmaster.

"Must it be here? I shouldn't like to be seen meeting with men outside the shop."

"O' course not." Tate scratched his neck, his mind running down the lanes to somewhere pleasant and secluded. "Meet me at the footbridge by the old mill."

"Okay. I'll be done by half five."

Her reservations made him nervous. Luckily she went back to reading the photo captions and he was able to leave with the flowers unseen.

He rested his foot on the low rung of the bridge. Half an hour to watch the sun extinguish itself behind the distant forest and to mull things over some more. Naturally, he wasn't rich, but there were now other directions in which to move. It taxed the brain, but Tate felt pride in his new-found authority over life. This is what it feels like to be a real man, he thought, reaching into his fresh pocket to retrieve an expensive cigar. But as he pushed his jaw forward, releasing the blue curlicues of smoke, he felt a sudden jolt of conscience. It hadn't occurred to him to alleviate his parents' problems. Much in suffering was his mother, from her corns; he could pay for a good doctor to sort it out. And his father didn't need convincing anymore that his mower was irreparable. The necklace was half theirs really, having been found on their premises. And besides, how could he explain all of this to them, the most steadfast of cynics?

Reflections made the river run an oily gold. Tate leant out over the bridge and felt the blood flowing fast to his head. A stench struck his nostrils so bad he recoiled, and in so doing he caught sight of a ragged black carcass hanging from the bridge's underside. Of course, there was that problem too. Deep, liquid shadows shape-shifted beneath floating seed pods and bubbles, and they momentarily took on the inverted spectre of Smyke. Tate felt his pocket for another smoke.

The snap of a broken twig brought him to attention. Advancing along the riverbank was the predatory hulk of Smyke, voice vibrating over the uneven ground,

"Tapping at my window – tip tip tap – TWO rook. And all others about my window tree."

Smyke still muttered to his border collie, long cold in the ground.

Tate watched the long-coated figure turning onto the bridge. Hooked from his crude rope belt were several freshly-killed rooks.

"Tell me, squib. Have y'dun it, and set 'em upon me?" Smyke moved towards him at a deranged pace. It was hard to tell what he wanted.

"Smart boy aren't cha," Smyke nodded at the suit. "Onta me are they?"

Tate shook his head, "I've not done it."

"No! Niver y'will till I do with ya!"

Perhaps it was his appearance, or his manner, but something enraged Smyke. The shotgun, which had been casually pointing downward, raised itself to Tate's chest, and Tate, who'd been subconsciously treading backwards, lost his footing at the end of the bridge. That's when he felt the stabbing in his chest. He staggered before falling and glimpsed a man grappling the farmer to the floor. Just before he went out, he caught the smell of her perfumed hair falling across his face.

Joy was sitting by his bed, peering at him nervously, when the nurse woke him. She looked very formal in matching coat, hat and gloves.

"How you feeling?"

"Hurts like hell when I move. Lucky really. He grazed me."

Tate's broken rib was firmly bandaged. They'd propped him with pillows and given him a side room so the police could speak with him privately. Through a gap in the door, he saw a restless man waiting in the corridor.

"Lucas?"

She smiled, "He was wonderful...knocking that beast to the ground..."

"He was with you then?"

She nodded, replaying the scene in her mind's eye, beaming with pride. Remembering herself, she looked up.

"What was it you wanted to tell me?"

All four walls were closing in on Tate. The bandage was tightening, crushing his ribcage; his organs were starting to perforate. Certain death. That's what he felt and wished for just then.

"Oh. Just that, me ma's got a basketful of ripe old cookers. They'll sell if you want 'em."

"Thank you."

He saw that she was keen to leave now and reassured her of his comfort. As she stood she looked quite the lady about town. The heels made all the difference.

"Joy?"

"Yes dear?"

"I hope you find everything you want in life."

"It's not as if I'm moving to America, Tate. No, I'm rather liking Nettlesby these days," she blew him a kiss.

The door closed. Settling his head he screwed his eyes to the bedside table, and there he saw the miniature roses standing in a jug of water.

***

Mr Morris, the-local-with-the-car, was anxious about time.

"Don't you worry Mrs Norwood. I'll take it slowly, steer round all them potholes," he said out of the car window, starting the engine. "What time does your train leave Leicester?"

"Ten to twelve," said Tate, easing himself into a comfortable position in the passenger seat.

The man checked his watch again, "I imagine you're still a bit tender. Make sure you've someone to help you with all that baggage at the other end."

"My cousin's meeting me. He's starting his own re-upholstery shop; I said I'd help him out."

"Where's that then?"

"Nottingham."

"That's good. You won't have to change."

Tate grinned. "I wouldn't say that," he said.

The sight of her son being swallowed up by the road might have got Edina Norwood all choked up; especially if she had been able to hear the car's dying breaths. But the rooks were particularly rambunctious that morning. They didn't allow for sentiment, living instantaneously and continuing as ever; bursting upwards from the trees in triumphant cacophony; wheeling down the valley with determination. They were on top of things, you see.

***

"A black cat crossing your path signifies that the animal is going somewhere."

Groucho Marx – comedian, actor, writer, 1890 - 1977

THE AGE OF THE RAT
Amy Blyth

*

London is in almost total darkness; the wind whistles off the
Thames, blowing great tides of rubbish across deserted streets, ush-
ering the stink of decay into every room in every building in every
street of the ruined metropolis. The rats venture slowly from their
various nests, stretching and yawning, flexing their long yellow teeth
in preparation for their feast. Some lie in huge piles of pink tails and
a mass of heaving fur, others claim solitary spots in empty dog beds
or dead children's cribs.

The pungent scent of the wind draws them from their respective
lairs; sharp noses point toward the starless sky; whiskers quiver in
anticipation. A sliver of fingernail moon illuminates their eager eyes;
the thousands of tiny glowing specs light up the dead roads just as
the human street lamps used to. The rats pause to savour the smell
of their new decaying kingdom.

All over the city they emerge – scuttling from burnt buildings and
abandoned tower blocks, picking their way over the smashed glass
from car windows, squeezing from between the doors of motionless
tube trains. A long line of writhing shapes flow like a thick black
river across London Bridge; a lone male sits atop a statue in Trafal-
gar Square, like a sentry on watch and a cluster of young rats forage
through the Odeon in Covent Garden, dining on stale popcorn. As
the wind howls, a grotesquely swollen female, her belly full with
squirming offspring, waddles slowly from her bed of shredded hymn
books. She doesn't have to go far for her evening meal – St Paul's

45

Cathedral is still full of the shrunken corpses of its last congregation who gathered when the final sickness swept the land.

The rats move leisurely though the streets, their scaly dragon tails trailing across ancient cobbles. They stop occasionally to scratch their bloated bodies and to groom their sleek black heads. There are no longer any footsteps to send them scuttling, nor high-pitched screams to set them cowering under floorboards or in underground drains. No suspicious crumbs of food are left poised in metal traps or laced with lethal powder. Now the creatures take their pick from the shelves of ransacked supermarkets, balancing on powerful hind legs to sniff the sugary offerings; they climb deftly like trapeze artists onto kitchen counters and gnaw their way through half eaten meals in deserted restaurants.

A tapping like the dripping of a leaky faucet is the only sound in Westminster as tiny feet gallop over the dusty pickets and forgotten banners that carpet the entire stretch of pavement from Parliament Square to the open gates of Downing Street. The rats pay no attention to what is left of their former ruler's final protest. They ignore the warnings sprawled on useless placards and the dying words painted onto the walls of Parliament.

The rats continue to feed.

"I care not much for a man's religion whose dog and cat
are not the better for it."

Abraham Lincoln – 16th President of the United States of America
(1861 -1865), 1809 – 1865

THREE TWATS AND A DOG TURD
WTA Mackewn

A loafer covering a sockless left foot stepped through the door of an East London pub and onto its bare wooden floor. The shoe was out of place, as was the foot, and the addition of its right sided companion only served to heighten the sense of awkwardness. The locals all stared, a mixture of angry working and non-working class eyes wished the foot and its accompanying human unimaginable ills. Fortunately for the foot's brain it was completely oblivious to the menacing silence of its surroundings or how out of place it and the other appendages actually were. The brain was far more worried about the safety of the single-geared fixie bike padlocked to the railings outside.

An androgynous squeal shattered the quiet and the eyes all slid back to their pints of Stella. Christopher, the owner of the brain and foot, forgot all about the bike and lolloped over to a table in the corner where a pair of other *individuals* in identical loafers sat.

"Look at what the heck has been written about *me*," said Christopher and slammed a two-day-old copy of the Guardian in the middle of the table.

"Whoa, Christophenia what's the dealio?" said Tarquinius (real name Geoff); a man who had decided that turquoise leggings showed that extra bit of imagination that one could never achieve in regular trousers.

"Just look at it," said Christopher.

Tarquinius had a Game Boy tied around his neck to prove how retro he was. It clattered against the table as he leaned forward to pick up the paper, almost spilling the half pint of cider he had been nursing for forty minutes. He was a man who feigned astonishment at everything, thereby hiding any real sense of ever being

49

impressed and letting his cool down. However, the fact that Christopher had managed to make it into the Guardian was something that turned his girly expressions of OMFG into a genuine squeal of delight.

It turned out, however, that when Tarquinius opened the paper to look at the offending article it was a printed scrap of A4 sellotaped rather carelessly to the middle of page seven. Instead of being disappointed by his friend's gut-wrenching pretentiousness, Tarq decided that Christopher must be being ironic. Of course just in case Christopher wasn't he decided not to draw attention to it.

The article turned out to be from an insignificant blogger named Retrowestside9mm_vintage-boi about how awful a recent synth recital Christopher had been in was. Tarquinius couldn't be bothered to read the whole thing, but as he skimmed down the page he did manage to make out a good number of words like talentless, pretentious, unforgivably sloppy, and finally, most disturbing of all, *predictable and banal.*

"O.M.F.G. What a total retardios. Who is this bozo anyway?" Tarquinius had long since given up swearing, as had the rest of them, it was far too passé.

"I don't know but Thom, like, knows where he lives so we're going to make this bozo pay," said Christopher.

"Oh yer totally," agreed Hen, a female with a touch of pseudohermaphroditism about her who was sitting opposite Tarquinius.

Hen was a girl who spent most of her time trying to perfect the art of pouting and looking nonchalant at the same time. She pouted at Christopher, who pouted back, then tried to look nonchalant, then pouted again, then adjusted his glasses, then pouted again. It had become their way of flirting, since actual flirting meant showing more than a cursory interest in someone and, showing more than a cursory interest in anything was in no way vintage or retro. Christopher flopped down on the sofa next to Hen and commenced more nonchalant pouting. Tarquinius recognised exactly what was going on and so interrupted,

"Let's set fire to his house."

The moment was shattered and Christopher looked over at Tarq. Hen, not wanting to let Tarquinius steal her limelight, came up with her own shocking plan,

"Cool yer, or we could, like, spike something he ate with, like, totally out there, hot chili sauce."

There was more silence and Tarquinius stared at Hen with

as much venom as he could muster. He really had no idea what Christopher saw in her. She was stupid, as that last statement had proved; she had a tendency to be enthusiastic about things and, worst of all, she wore new clothes. Nothing that ever covered her stick form had come from a market or charity shop, it was all Adidas or Nike and bought in a shop. She wasn't retro; she was netro and without doubt should not be hanging out with a visionary like Christopher. A man so great he had practically invented the whole Utah Disco/Funkadelia look that had been so big the previous summer.

"I think maybe the house burning is a bit extreme yah? And, like, it might just, like, have too high a carbon footprint. I want my revenge to be, like, totally enviro?"

"Oh yer totally," said Tarquinius, who was leaning so far forward that his Game Boy slipped off the table and into Christopher's lap. He stumbled an apology of sorts and shuffled back into his seat.

Christopher frowned at Tarquinius; the need for acceptance flew headlong in the face of everything they stood for. They were *all* meant to be individuals. They were meant to stick two retro-clad fingers up at the drones who polluted the world with their conformist attitudes. They were meant to revel in the magic that was crunk. They were meant to... Christopher's thoughts trailed off as it suddenly occurred to him that Tarquinius could fancy him. Unfortunately the dress code and demeanor of any self-respecting individual made determining sexual preference almost impossible. Christopher was just considering whether it would be uncool to ask when Hen interrupted,

"How about we like throw dog mess at his house?"

"Oh, like, yeh," said Tarquinius scoffing, "like, we'll get it all over our hands and stuff? Hen you're so, like, thick sometimes."

"Well, like, I didn't mean literally obviously."

"What so you'd like to do it existentially then I suppose?" Tarquinius smiled to himself having got a five-syllable word into the conversation.

"And how the hell would I existentially cover the house in it?"

"Well Hen, I don't know that's the point."

"Look I'm just thinking out loud here, you know, trying to bring some imagination to table, yeh? So if my thoughts aren't fully formed when they come to the surface that's because I'm like, you know, orally sketching."

"It sounds a lot like just being as thick as pig shit to me."

Silence.

"Ok guys let's just take five for a second. Tarquinius I think you need to just chill out a bit yeh?" said Christopher.

"Whatever." He slumped back into his seat, bitter at the fact that Hen's stupidity had forced him to swear.

"Besides, I think that the dog mess idea has some legs. But, let's go for 'The. Old. Burning. Bag. Routine.'" Christopher paused to let the enormity of what he was saying sink in, and when he realised that his two companions were suitably sucked in he went on to explain.

"What you do is, you get some mess, put it in a bag then stick it on his doorstep, set fire to it and ring the door bell. Then when he comes out he thinks 'Oh no, there's like a fire on my door step or something!' and tries to, like, stamp on it to put it out or whatever. It's great because he, like, gets dog doo-doo all over his shoes. It was also totally big in the eighties and I think this bozo needs to be given a lesson..." Christopher pulled his glasses to the end of his nose and fixed Tarquinius and then Hen square in the eyes, "... a lesson with a 'vintage feel'."

Hen was so enthralled that she let out a little squeak and then followed through with a tiny round of applause. Tarquinius, however, was not so easily taken in,

"Yeh but, like, what if he like gets himself some water or whatever and, like, puts it out. Then he'd, like, have cleaned it up and put the fire out?"

"Ok, erm, so like, what do you suggest?"

Tarq was silent, he had no idea what to suggest and he didn't much like Christopher's tone. He opened his mouth to say as much but before he could, Hen interrupted.

"Like, why don't we, like, stick one of those totally retro and cool French bangers in the bag with the mess then when he opens the door, bang! Pebble dashed joy destroyer."

"Oh my god that's like totally it!"

Hen beamed at Christopher, Tarq glared at Hen, desperate to derail her monopoly over Christopher; then it came to him,

"And who do we know with a dog?"

"Triff," replied Hen without breaking eye contact with Christopher.

"OMFG! Triff? Are you honking serious? There's no way

we're getting it off her, she is like a total, like, whatever; isn't she Christopher?"

Forty-five minutes later a fleet of single geared bikes were being chained to a set of railings on Balham High Road. Christopher took the lead and approached the door to Triff's flat. He was not at all easy about it, the building was Victorian and he had no idea how the entry systems to anything other than a 1960s tower block functioned. Fortunately the building only contained two flats and, after irritating a man in his eighties, he got through to Triff and she buzzed to let them in.

"I'm, like, totally not going in there," said Tarquinius, who hadn't stopped scowling since they'd left Shoreditch.

"Why not?"

"Well because not only does she buy her clothes from, like, M&S or something, which should be enough of a reason, I, like, took a vow at the last crunk night I was at that I wouldn't, like, enter any bourgeois properties until June. It's kind of a spiritual detox thing."

Neither Hen nor Christopher had the energy to point out he'd spent the previous two evenings at his parent's Cotswold cottage, and so left him outside to guard the bikes.

Triff was standing in her hallway in a pair of jeans and T-Shirt.

"Hey Hen, long time n o speak, what are you doing...?"

Triff trailed off as she saw Christopher come into view.

"What's he doing here?"

"Yer, like, hi Triff, like, Christopher and I are just here to see, like, how you are, you know and catch up and stuff."

"And to, like, erm, borrow your dog?" said Christopher.

Hen elbowed Christopher in the ribs, but he had no idea why.

"Why do you want to borrow my dog?"

"Yer, what Christopher was saying is that since we haven't seen you in, like, *forever* we'd like to help you out by taking your dog for a walk."

Triff did not look convinced.

"Yer it's like a spiritual detox kind of thing, any friend I haven't seen in a long time I've, like, decided to do a good deed for."

"Right, and so why's he here?"

"Oh, like, he's here to, like, help me out or whatever."

"Well thanks for the offer but no."

Christopher was not used to people refusing him, "What do you mean no? Like, me and Hen we, like, come here offering our help and you don't want it? Like, what's that about, you really, like, erm...."

Triff cut him off, "No Christopher, if you were actually offering to help me I'd be delighted to accept, but there are several fairly obvious reasons why I know you're lying."

"Like what?" said Hen who had decided she didn't like Triff now that she had contradicted Christopher, the one and only pioneer of Utah Disco/Funkadelia.

"Well, like the fact that every time you lie your voice goes up about two octaves as it did just then, and, like, the fact that this arse is here offering to support you in one of your endeavors."

"Why's that so shocking? I'm known all over Shoreditch for my generous nature. People say like, 'look there's Christopher, he's, like, totally generous or whatever,' like, the whole time."

"Oh really, so what about the time Hen here OD'd on that Meow Meow you sold her and ended up on dialysis for a week?"

Hen went red, "Come on Triff, it wasn't, like, a whole week, just kind of, like, six days."

"You didn't come to see her once."

"I've got, like, a medically documented phobia of hospitals."

"And I suppose the time you borrowed that money and she got her gas cut off because she couldn't afford to pay the bill - that was all down your fear of cash machines?"

"No, actually it was because I was, like, boycotting the banking system after, like, the whole erm thing in the City."

"Oh right."

"Jeez Hen, your friend is a bit of a Nazi."

And with that Triff slammed the door.

Back outside Tarquinius was brooding. What was it that Hen had that he didn't? She was quite obviously sub-humanly stupid, the way she hospitalised herself on Meow Meow was testament to that: her synth playing was utterly awful and she wore Chanel No. 5 for Christ's sake. It just wasn't possible to wear a perfume ironically, which meant that she really thought the stuff was cool. It was enough to make anyone sick; except for Christopher. Before he could ponder the matter any further they reappeared on the street.

"So, like, where's the dog?"

"Oh well we ran into a few problems there."

54

"Was her stupid friend not in then?"

"No she was there; she just wouldn't let us have the dog."

"Well there's a surprise! Hen's friends are as dull as she is."

"Hey!"

"OMFG would you two just give it a rest already. Now I've come up with a new plan. What we'll do is we'll wait here until Triff comes out and then we secretly follow her down to the park and then we can like snatch the dogs stuff when it's done its business."

"What? Well why can't we just go down to the park now and get some? This is South London; the place will be full of it."

"Jeeze Tarq, getting some unknown dog stuff from an unknown dog? That's like totally unhygienic; we could get Hepatitis or something."

Tarquinius couldn't quite see the logic there, but he was willing to admit that Christopher was a fair bit more intelligent than he was and so bowed to his superior medical knowledge. He did, however, have one question,

"So we'll all wait here until she comes out? Like, won't that take a while?"

"Could do, that's why we're going to do it in shifts, Hen and I drew straws while we were in there and both got long ones, which means that you've got the first shift."

Tarq could see from the expression on Christopher's face that this wasn't up for discussion.

"What, well where are you going?"

"The pub, see you in three hours."

The next day the three of them were standing on another pavement, this time back in their beloved East London. Opposite them was their intended target, a shabby Georgian townhouse with a black front door and a poster advertising a WAREHOWZ RAVE for the 31st September.

"So who's doing it then?" said Tarq.

"Well, I thought you would," said Hen.

"Why should I? I had to fight your orangutan of a friend for the bloody stuff. And let me tell you, wrestling a woman in a park at dusk does not go down well with the public; I thought I was going to get lynched or something."

"Well I had to, like, get the bangers."

"Look would you two just shut up yeh? I'll do it." This had been Christopher's plan all along; whilst he saw himself as far too important to carry out any of the leg work he was more than happy to take the final moment of glory. And this was going to be glorious indeed.

He took the paper bag from Tarquinius and the banger from Hen and walked calmly across the single lane of road. Ringing the door bell of his critic's house he bent down and placed the banger under the bag, clicked open his Harley Davidson Zippo, lit the fuse and ran back to watch.

The door opened and the retrowestside9mm_vintage-boi poked his head out. He looked from left to right to see who had rung, and not noticing the bag on the doorstep, withdrew his head and shut the door.

Christopher was incensed and ran back across the road to the door; the banger had obviously failed and whilst he would never have described himself as violent he was not going to let the issue lie. He would throw the damn bag through the window and be done with it.

He picked up the bag and had just enough time to register a hissing sound before the fuse hit the gunpowder.

Bang.

"If all the beasts were gone, men would die from a great loneliness of spirit, for whatever happens to the beasts also happens to the man. All things are connected. Whatever befalls the Earth befalls the sons of the Earth."

Chief Seattle of the Suquamish Tribe, 1786 – 1866, letter to President Franklin Pierce

HENRIETTA AND THE CROW
Christina Thompson

Henrietta Block had been waiting for nearly an hour; eyes peeking furtively between the sliver of her blinds so as not to draw the attention of the large black crow perched on the treetop across the way. She suspected this was the same bird that had struck at her the day before last and the day before that too. She hadn't left the small one-bedroom apartment since the first assault, except once to dash out to the library to see when she was due for her next shift. Henrietta much preferred going in to see the roster than to call in, and so she always did.

The crow cocked its smooth head in her direction and Henrietta held her breath for all of ten seconds before she gave herself permission to inhale once again, a short quick intake, and felt the gentle flutter in her stomach as she frantically thought of an escape.

 It was Wednesday and she was soon due for her shift at the library where she'd worked part-time for nearly a year. She loved when her supervisor, Tom Bagley, all tall and gangly with boyish looks, assigned her to the children's department, allowing her to take part in storytime, entertaining the few children that actually showed with Nelly and Sasha the puppets.

Three days had gone by since the first incident. She'd been coming back from the grocers, bags in hand, when she'd suddenly felt something swooping down at her from above, the sound of fluttering wings, and had bolted to the front entrance of the apartment building in a panic, screaming in a high-pitched squeal.

Albert, the concierge, had been smoking outside in the courtyard at the time, and followed her in to the lobby to see what was the matter.

- You alright there, Mrs Block?

He tried hard to stifle his laughter at the sight of her, wide-eyed and disheveled hair, taking in her terror and shock. She was usually so carefully coiffed, it took him a second to keep himself in check and respond with as much finesse as he could muster.

- Looks like you got quite the scare.

Henrietta quickly wiped the tears that had started forming at the corners of her eyes and snapped out of her trance.

- Did you see that thing attack me?
- It was just a crow, nothing to be afraid of. He must have thought you had some food or something. Strange behaviour but then it's been a long winter and it must be hard to get some grub.

Henrietta had waited two long minutes for the elevator, not trusting her legs to get her up the stairs to the fourth-floor apartment, and her legs still shook when she let herself fall onto her sofa chair with a thump. It wasn't till she'd soaked in a long hot bath, sipped three cups of her favourite chamomile and lavender tea and listened to Ravel's 'Pavane pour une infante défunte' that she started to feel the calming effects soothe her nerves and almost convince her that she'd forgotten the whole ordeal.

She'd slept fitfully that night; dreams of a vicious bird cloaked in black feathers swooping down at her with several strikes as it dive-bombed and followed her halfway through the park. She'd woken suddenly when the assailant pecked at her head. As her eyes regained focus, she felt a light nudge from Terence, her spotted tabby, gently coercing her out of bed.

While Terence ate noisily from his dried food bowl, Henrietta stared out the kitchen window and watched a family of starlings flutter from branch to branch. Determined not to let the previous day's events disrupt the even cadence she'd managed to create for herself, she methodically jumped straight into the day's tasks: laundry, watering the plants, ironing shirts, sweeping and mopping the floors. After all the chores had been done, and the whole chicken she'd brought home the day before was stuffed and baking in the oven, she put herself to the pleasures of the weekend: listened to her radio program *Writers & Company*, made a selection of rhymes to bring to the following reading, curled up on the couch with a glass of Chardonnay and the latest bestseller in hand for a quiet evening by herself.

Henrietta managed to do all this in the blissful comfort of her own home. Life had moved in this way for quite some time, without major ebb or flow, but at a steady meandering pace that comforted her and made her feel that all was good. High from a day well spent, she slept peacefully that night.

The next morning, she rose early and with a bounce to her step, ate a poached egg on toast and skipped down the stairs to go to the municipal library.

As soon as she set foot out of doors, she heard the low squawk of a nearby crow. She lifted a weary eye to the treetops and quickened her pace, her heart stepping up a rate as she cut across the street and quickly hopped the bus that was conveniently waiting by the bus shelter. She found herself looking after the bird, even as the bus rode up to her stop. Finding strength in numbers, she merged with the throng of passengers getting off at the library, and made way to the front desk.

Tom Bagley, the head librarian, was there today, in his trademark corduroys and V-neck cardigan. He stood up rather suddenly as she approached the counter, and self-consciously adjusted his glasses.

- Ah Nettie, come to check when you're due next?

He had the annoying habit of calling her "Nettie," something he no doubt considered to be a term of endearment and that she didn't dare dispute. Still, it made her uneasy, particularly when he said it in front of staff. Tom was undeterred and kept up a lively and chatty tone whenever she was around.

Henrietta paid him little heed and jotted down the next two weeks schedule in her little notebook. As she turned to leave she found he was casually blocking her way.

- I put you on for storytime again...
- Yes, I got that, thank you.

His eyes searched hers for a moment longer, hoping to make contact with some part of her but she appeared unmoved and so he made way for her to pass.

- See you tomorrow then.

And off she went. She felt like a young girl, moving swiftly back to familiar territory, away from the disturbing feelings that arose whenever Tom Bagley was around. She didn't want anything to disturb the quiet place she'd come to since moving back home, and whenever he loomed near, she felt a strange pull that she was determined to nip in the bud.

Full of vague thoughts of Tom Bagley and what she was going to do for the next presentation, she stopped at a local coffee shop for a café latte, and let the afternoon hours dwindle away as she browsed through magazines and read the daily newspaper.

The sun was low when she neared the exterior of her apartment building and she instinctively looked this way and that to make sure the coast was clear. Dark silhouettes were hard to make out against the darkened sky but she thought she saw something rustle up above. She walked at a quick pace toward the front door and was almost halfway when she was surprised by the sudden swoop of a large crow that made for her and gave a sharp blow to the back of her neck. Henrietta screamed and started to run. The crow dropped once again from its perch and scraped its talons into the back of her head.

She stopped dead in her tracks and with a piercing scream, covered her head with both arms. This did nothing to deter the bird, in fact it seemed to fuel its attack as it dove at her again and again and pecked the top of her head. All of this happened in a matter of seconds and Henrietta soon woke out of her stupor and made a mad dash for the door once again. As she slammed the door shut and ran up the short flight of stairs and fumbled with her key to open the main door to the lobby, she heard the loud caw-aw-ah of her attacker. Her palms were sweaty, her heart raced and she was aware of a slight buzzing in her ear and a dull pain in the back of her head.

She placed an ice-pack to the back of her head and lay back on the couch. Her mind raced as she tried to imagine ever being able to leave her house again.

The next day, she called in sick. She was relieved when one of the other librarians, Kate, answered the phone, saving her from another awkward conversation with Tom. She felt embarrassed and terrified at the same time and found the only thing she could do was to hide out on the couch all day, watching soap operas and sitcom repeats.

She dreamed of a river, dark and cold, and having to swim her way across while strange slimy things rubbed against her legs. At the other side of the riverbank, she was greeted by a man wearing a long black coat. He took her in his arms and said: 'I will blow your mind.' Men danced in feathered cloaks at a raging office party and as she slipped away from the crowd she bumped into her old friend Tom Bagley. He pulled her by the hand and twirled her around. She was giddy and dizzy and felt a tingling in her nerve endings as he planted his lips on hers and gave her a kiss. She was spun around and found herself standing in a circle of crows. The birds stared at her with beady eyes, moving their heads in quick jolted movements. She felt they were trying to say something to her but she couldn't quite make out the words above the cacophony of cawing.

Henrietta woke to the sound of Terence scratching at the bottom of his empty bowl. She flung the goose-down duvet aside and climbed out of bed with the beginnings of what was to be a low-grade headache. Terence ran over and brushed up against her legs, purring in anticipation of being fed.

She sat in silence at the kitchen table, cup of coffee in hand, wondering at her dreams, and more importantly how she was going to face the day. She felt antsy about calling in sick a second time yet could see no way around it. She decided to postpone making any big decisions and went for a long hot shower instead. Once her hair was dry, her eye makeup carefully applied and she was dressed to go, she lost courage and opted to make a phone call.

She dialed and waited, tracing the square-numbered buttons on the phone with her finger, when a familiar voice suddenly answered.

- It's Henrietta. I'm still not feeling that well today and was thinking I wouldn't come in this morning.

There was a long silence before Tom Bagley answered.

- Kate's down with the flu and Martha had to bring her son to the clinic for his bronchitis. I could really use the help. What's the matter?

She mumbled something '...well okay, it's not that bad, I just thought I'd wait another day to get better but if you need me... I'll come in,' to which he gave a cheerful 'You're a star' and hung up. She felt a bit sick to her stomach.

And so she paced back and forth several times, peering out from behind the blinds at the large black crow perched on the treetop across the way. It seemed to be patiently waiting, its gaze fixed on something in the distance. She moved away from the window to don her coat, hat and mitts, and wanting to gage its intentions and whereabouts one last time before venturing out, she peeked out again only to realize that the crow was gone. She seized the moment and rushed through the door, and down the flight of stairs.

She walked into the courtyard a little more quickly than she'd planned and walked at a steady determined pace. Not a branch stirred and she found that even with small quick glimpses over her shoulder she couldn't see the bird in question. She waited nervously at the bus stop, leaning out on several occasions to see if it was coming up the road. When the bus finally arrived, she got on and found a seat at the back.

Tom greeted her with a gruff 'You're late.' She looked away in embarrassment, muttered an apology and hung her coat before efficiently going about her business on the library floor.

During the course of her day, she found herself circling near the service desk more often than necessary, in the hope of catching Tom's eye; wanting to make sure that he wasn't cross with her. She'd always been conscientious and beyond reproach yet it seemed her recent behaviour had somehow created a gap she hadn't the faintest idea how to rectify. The best she could do was to work even more diligently, which she did quite well. Storytime was a success, she had replaced Kate as head storyteller and was overjoyed when the children laughed at the right moment and she caught Tom's approving nod.

A few hours later, while she was re-shelving in the Alternative Health aisle, Tom approached.

- Ah Henrietta, just the person I wanted to see. Would you be able to lock up for me tonight?

Henrietta flushed uncontrollably under his stare, she hadn't realized his eyes were dark blue, and at that moment, seemed capable of boring into her very being.

- Yes, of course, no problem.
- You're feeling better?

A flash of embarrassment and the not-so-unpleasant flutter in the pit of her stomach, reminiscent of the delicious kiss he'd planted on her lips last night.

- I am, thank you.
- Good. Come see me later, I'll show you the code for the alarm.

He rested his hand on her shoulder and broke into his boyish smile. She found herself drawn to the fine lines at the edges of his eyes, small wrinkles that contrasted with his youthful zeal.

The library was nearly empty. Henrietta locked the doors behind the last member and did the rounds before close. When it came time for Tom to show her how to lock up, she was most attentive and found herself leaning in closely to be near him.

- And then you punch in the numbers and wait to see it start to count down.

She detected a light spicy fragrance, he must have put on a fresh splash of men's cologne. The last of the interns put on her coat and waved them both good night. Tom soon followed suit.

- Call me on my cell if you run into any problems.

Henrietta nodded dutifully, wanting very much to keep his trust. She followed him to the door in order to lock up behind him.

- Henrietta, thanks again.

She beamed back at him, almost missing the fact that he'd used her full name. The lock turned with a loud clunk.

It had begun to snow. She watched him dash across the road and wave at someone in that direction. She moved in close to the window to follow his trajectory when she suddenly saw who he was waving at. She was tall and slender, and wore a long bright tangerine ladies' coat and a smart beret, with dark curls falling passed her shoulders. Tom rested his hand in the small of her back, gesturing for her to move ahead.

Henrietta stood for a long time at the window, long after they'd both dropped out of sight. She felt slightly foolish and an unfamiliar tightening in her throat.

When she stepped outside the library, light flurries filled the night air; the wind stirred, and drove snowflakes against the windowpanes of city cars. Snow began to settle in the contours of Henrietta's hair, round the collar of her coat. She walked along the river that divided the north and south banks of the city; trees silhouetted against the twilight sky. But Henrietta did not see this nor did she see the band of crows congregating at the tops of the small group of trees in the park along the way. She walked for almost an hour, taking small streets to avoid the glaring city lights, and was surprised when she arrived in front of her own building.

For a moment, she stopped at the front entrance and looked back at the branches that had terrified her so that very morning. They stood empty before the snow-filled sky.

She put the key in the lock and made her way up the stairs to her apartment, feeling every bit as foolish and as numb as she had once been when disappointed as a young girl. Standing in front of her door, she took a deep breath and vowed to leave such silly things behind her now. She ventured forth into her apartment, the one place of true solace, and looked forward to the predictable calm ebb of night.

Notes:

1. Superstition abounds when it comes to deciphering omens. In 'Animal Speak: Understanding Animal Messengers, Totems, and Signs,' author Ted Andrews talks about what he calls animal medicine, and how every encounter with a living creature can become an epiphany of the heart — as well as a message from the divine. "Terrestrial animals have always had a strong symbology associated with them. They have represented the emotional side of life, often reflecting qualities that must be overcome, controlled, and/or re-expressed. They are also symbols of power – powers associated with the invisible realm that we can learn to manifest within the visible." *Animal Speak: Understanding Animal Messengers, Totems, and Signs, written by Ted Andrews.*

2. "Most European traditions view the crow as bad omens, problems and death. However, many Amerindian tribes believed Crow was both keeper of the sacred law and trickster, and an omen of transformation. Crow has no sense of time and lives in the Void, having the ability to the past, present and future at the same time. Along with Coyote and Raven, Crow is considered a trickster and a shape-shifter." Taken from *Suite101: Crow, Mysterious Pagan Symbol: Sign of Law, Creation, Magick, Prophecy, Cunning and Trickery http://www.suite101.com/content/crow-mysterious-pagan-symbol-a20797#ixzz181sljCfT*

3. "If you talk to the animals they will talk with you and you will know each other. If you do not talk to them, you will not know them, and what you do not know, you will fear. What one fears, one destroys." *Animal Speak: Understanding Animal Messengers, Totems, and Signs, citation by Chief Dan George*

"Don't approach a goat from the front, a horse from the back,
or a fool from any side."

Yiddish Proverb

WAVE GOODBYE
Rebecca Jenkins

The Maldivian capital Malé, a favourite touchdown for newlyweds seeking white sand and turquoise water backdrops for their cookie-cutter honeymoon albums, was an undeniably odd starting point for her sabbatical (at twenty-eight, Talitha thought herself too old to call it a "gap year"). But it wasn't until she saw her destination on the departure board at Heathrow, the accent missing from above the 'e', that she considered the irony of choosing a destination eponymous with the very thing that had necessitated the break in the first place. Still, she wasn't going to get all superstitious about it. A name was a name. It wasn't a sign or anything.

As it turned out, her stay on Malé was short-lived. Two days into the conservation project, Talitha met an Australian girl called Sarah, whose boyfriend of about two hours, convinced them that counting turtles in the Maldives was far too 2003. The place to be at, according to Matt, was Galle in Sri Lanka, and by a not so remark-able coincidence he'd already booked his ride there the following day. They needed volunteers at an elephant sanctuary where daily meals were provided for six four-hour shifts per week, and a friend of Matt's ran a hostel where they could stay for free if they helped with cooking and whatnot over the busy Christmas period. Talitha agreed to go, simply because she couldn't think of any reason not to. And besides, she liked Sarah.

The crossing was choppy. The girls heaved below deck while Matt, shirtless and apparently unaffected by the unrelenting rise and fall, sank beers with a bunch of Aussie guys Talitha assumed he knew from home but whom she later discovered he'd met aboard. Sarah, she suspected, too, had that knack, endemic to Australians, of befriending strangers in the unlikeliest circumstances. For the journey though at least, Talitha had Sarah to herself. They shared Alka-Seltzer and stories of travels and boyfriends past.

It was Matt who first commented on the similarity between the girls. They were frequently mistaken for sisters, increasingly more so as the fierce sun sprinkled a dusting of freckles across Talitha's English rose complexion, and her ash-blonde highlights flamed as golden as those in Sarah's shoulder skimming waves. Both only children, they were secretly pleased at the sibling inference, though Talitha was painfully aware that the likeness didn't extend beyond the physical.

Sarah was like the Duracell Bunny; after a double dung-shovelling shift she could call on her apparently bottomless energy reserves to frolic on the beach while the sun was still up, host an impromptu gathering for her ever-expanding collection of friends as it went down, and sink her bodyweight in margaritas as the moon joined the party (expressing disappointment or outrage – depending on the volume of margaritas drunk – if ever Talitha hinted at bowing out). She'd retire eventually, typically a few hours before the poo collecting recommenced, but judging by the sounds that bled from Sarah and Matt's room during those siestas, power napping wasn't the secret to Sarah's Stepford Wives meets Baywatch Nights approach to life.

"Hey hon, you look tired. You ok?" Sarah asked regularly. Talitha wanted to reply that exhaustion was a fairly typical physiological reaction from a person barely surviving on three hours sleep a night. "Yeah I'm fine. Might try to get my head down for an hour or so after dinner."

"Oh, you're not coming on the night dive?"

Christmas day was approaching and Sarah was planning a party. "Noah said we can stay on at the sanctuary after work and set up camp on the riverbank. Chill with a few bottles of wine and watch the sun go down," she said.

"Noah?" asked Talitha.

"Yeah, Noah," replied Sarah. "He'll be there too – you don't mind, do you?"

"No, I mean who's Noah?"

"You know. The elephant dude. Caretaker of the sanctuary. I introduced you the other day. Lovely guy. Toothy."

"Dr Fang," Matt piped up from the sofa where he was cradling a beer. "Or should that be Dr Dolittle? Funny little fella."

"Why do you call him Dr Dolittle?" Talitha asked.

"Well he's kind of got this weird thing going down with the Nellies. A special connection. In other words, he's a nut job," Matt snorted. "Oh right, I see," said Talitha. "Dr Dolittle. Because 'Noah' doesn't have enough of an animal association already." Matt stared blankly. "Huh?" She hadn't meant to snap and was about to say so when Sarah laughed.

"Oh Tal, you've got to remember not everyone's as smart as you." She tugged gently on Talitha's ponytail and handed Matt another beer.

Talitha was pretty sure Sarah hadn't introduced her to the toothy caretaker, and this was confirmed when, working her first shift without Sarah who'd gone wreck diving with Matt, he appeared on her patch. "Noah," he said, pointing at his chest and flashing his unsightly dentures. "Welcome Sri Lanka. You like?" He suggested Talitha hang up her shovel and accompany him to the bathhouse to help hose down Roger, the newest resident of the sanctuary, an adult male who'd recently been rescued from the wild with gunshot wounds to his face.

"No more see," he gestured at Roger's right eye.

"That's terrible," replied Talitha.

Talitha unravelled the hosepipe as Noah, tiptoeing even on his footstool, began to scrub. Roger wasn't straining against his ankle chains the way the babies did when the volunteers did the bathing. He nuzzled Noah's chamois, seemingly loving the attention. Roger was to Noah what the world and his wife were to Sarah, thought Talitha.

Christmas Day and Sarah had stockpiled enough Corona and Pinot Grigio to sink an ark. Talitha suspected the riverside party was going to watch the sun come up as well as go down. Despite her exhaustion, she was looking forward to it. The numbers had dwindled to a manageable five – her, Sarah and Matt, Noah and Aaron, the elusive, dreadlocked hostel owner who'd barely said two words to Talitha since she arrived. Still, it was Christmas, thought Talitha. Goodwill to all men, even those of the stoned Australian variety.

Their shift ended and Sarah and Talitha between them manoeuvred the supplies across the suntrap plain, looking forward to immersing themselves in the cool jets of the river at the north of the compound. They stripped to their two pieces in the shade of the frangipani trees and waded out. Sarah had the idea of using the river as a makeshift cool box and they wedged their buckets between those boulders closest to the bank. They spread out the multicoloured throw donated by Aaron and weighted down two diagonal corners with gas lamps to light later.

"Cute," said Talitha, surveying their work.

"Happy Christmas, babe," said Sarah, gesturing for Talitha to sit. "What would Madame like to drink?"

"Madame would like a glass of your finest wine."

Sarah pulled a bottle out of the river and peered at the label. "One Styrofoam cup of vintage 2001 screw-top Pinot Grigio coming up."

As predicted the party had barely started by sundown. Aaron arrived last, lugging a clay pot of still steaming dhal. "Merry Crimbo, everyone," he said. "Shall I do the honours?" he reached into his bag and pulled out a packet of Rizlas.

In the time it took for the first joint to pass around, the blood-orange sky faded to a milky blue. Sarah and Talitha cleared the empties, refilled cups and lit the lamps. "Toast," Sarah suggested as she sat back down. "To us!"

"To us!" everyone chorused.

"To new friends," said Noah.

"To new friends!"

"To new beginnings," said Talitha.

"To new beginnings!"

It was gone three when they called it a night. Talitha re-alised she and Sarah had been together every waking moment of Christmas Day without either mentioning family or loved ones. No calls were made, no text messages sent. After repeated stumbling embraces and pledges of eternal friendship, the group said goodbye to Noah. "So long, Dr Dolittle," Matt slurred as his silhouette disap-peared out of gaslight range. "Shush!" squealed Talitha and Sarah in unison. "Oh like he'd understand," said Matt.

"If we could walk with the animals,

Talk to the animals,

Grunt and squeak and I forgot the other word with the animals," he sang.

"You're hilarious Matt."

Darkness was ebbing away by the time Talitha slipped under the covers. She could have sworn she'd only just fallen asleep when Sarah, showered and dressed, stuck her head around the door. "Hon, Matt and I are going diving for the day. Wanna come?"

"What time is it?"

"Just after six. You wanna come? We can wait while you shower and stuff?"

"Nah, it's ok. Have a good one. See you tonight."

"Ok darl. Sweet dreams."

She dozed for an hour or so then decided to make the most of a day to herself, packed a paperback, SPF and a flask of iced tea and headed to the elephant sanctuary where she'd perch on the hilltop and chill out under the acacias.

The plain was deserted; no elephants or staff in sight. She was lost in Ruth Rendell when she sensed a presence, looked up and saw a figure emerge from the entrance to the compound. He was striding directly towards her. She sat up and shielded her eyes from the sun. It was Noah. "Sarah," he called. "Sarah!"

"No, it's Talitha," she shouted, rising to her feet, adjusting her sarong. "What's up?"

"Come. Quick," he ordered, turning on his heels and marching back in the direction he'd come from. He looked over his shoulder to ensure she had obeyed. "Come," he said again when he saw she was still standing there.

"What's up?" she asked again, stuffing her things into her bag and running to catch up with him. "What is it?"

He was moving so quickly now she was jogging to keep up with him. "Something wrong. Elephants gone," he said gesturing at the empty plain.

"Gone? What do you mean, gone? Gone where?"

"Up," he said, stopping so Talitha could catch her breath. "Come, Sarah," he said, striding off again.

"Hang on. Wait," she called after him. "Up?" she asked, "Up where? When? What do you mean?"

"Come," said Noah again. "Please. I say to you on the way." He looked back at her and she caught a flash of something in his eyes she couldn't pinpoint. She heard her mother's voice in her head. *How well do you know this man?*

The road beyond the compound was breaking into its morning chorus, the clackety-clack of the coconut sellers setting up stall and the squawk of ticket touts circling their prey. Reneging on his promise of an explanation, Noah had flagged down a tuk-tuk and began what sounded like a heated discussion with the driver. She opened her mouth and waited for the chance to get a word in, but Noah beat her to it. "You have money?" She fished in her bag and pulled out a clutch of Rupees. "One, two, three, four hundred," she counted. "Alrighto," he ushered her into the back of the tuk-tuk and he and the driver recommenced their breakneck exchange as they pulled away.

"Sarah, where your friend is?" he turned to her eventually.

"I'm Talitha. Sarah went diving. Early this morning. Why?"

"Something wrong. Elephants gone. Mean something wrong."

"Like what?" Talitha shouted over the engine as it chugged uphill. Noah leaned forward and said something which made the driver come to an abrupt halt. He handed over her fistful of notes and gestured for her to get out. Her watch said it was only just after nine. "We wait here," Noah said, looking around.

"Wait for what?" asked Talitha, but she wasn't sure Noah knew either. A hundred metres or so along the mountain road they found a restaurant. Talitha left Noah talking to the owner as she went to the ladies' room to splash her face. When she emerged Noah was alone on the veranda, shielding his eyes as he scanned the panorama. Talitha felt in her bag but remembered she'd left her camera at the hostel. Shame. They had a glorious view over the elephant sanctuary and the river where they'd partied the previous evening, and beyond that the wide sweep of golden sand separated from the coastal road by a row of palms and a rainbow of fishing boats. The beach looked busy. Strangely so for this time of day. The owner reappeared and handed Noah a black case. He took out a pair of binoculars and fiddled with the dials, turning them slowly as he swept over the panorama with a slow, fluid arc. Looking for his elephants, she thought. "Can I?" asked Talitha. Noah handed her the binoculars and showed her how to zoom in and out. She focused on the activity on the beach. The tide was out. Really, really far out, she noted as she inched north. "Something wrong with sea," Noah said as though he'd heard her thoughts. She twigged what the activity was: the receding shoreline promised the fishermen the catch of a lifetime. "Weird," she said, handing the binoculars back to Noah. "Elephants know," he said, looking around as if one might appear and tell them what was going on. "Let's get a drink," Talitha suggested, growing impatient. They ordered papaya juice and handed the binoculars back and forth between sips. "So has anything like this happened before?" asked Talitha, unsure of what exactly "this" was but aware by now of the futility of asking Noah to explain his behaviour. When he didn't answer she followed his gaze to the horizon. They didn't need the binoculars to see the swirl of water returning to the shoreline. And even from this distance she could see it was coming in too quickly. Those fishermen were going to get wet, she thought. She looked through the viewfinder. It was still coming in. Way, way too quickly, the strip of sand fast disappearing. Noah stood up. "Come," he said.

Each time he slowed for her to catch him up, he galloped off downhill again as soon as she was alongside him. On flip-flopped foot, the mountain road seemed to snake with greater frequency than it had during their tuk-tuk's ascent. Rounding another sharp curve Talitha found herself alongside Noah. A bus had stopped, its engine still running, the passengers hanging over the balustrades of the roadside viewing bay, apparently preoccupied with something going on below. An American voice stood out from the otherwise indistinguishable hum. A man. "Oh Jesus. Look at that wave. Oh God. Oh God no." One more step to the side of the road and that's when she saw.

She hadn't known what she'd been expecting until she saw what it was she hadn't. The American's words had momentarily conjured up images of Kate Winslet and Leonardo DiCaprio, running down the corridors of the Titanic as frothy chlorine-clean water gushed around their heels. But this was something else. Something else altogether. Only the roofs on the coastal strip below were visible, bobbing like croutons in the scrap yard soup swirling around them. The water was a thick meaty stock, barely visible for its assortment of sorry ingredients. Among the unidentifiable, Talitha noted a fishing boat, a refrigerator, a motorcycle, a canary-yellow surfboard. "Boat, fridge, bike, board," she said to herself. "Boat, fridge, bike, board." It was like that game show where you had to remember all the things on the conveyor belt. "Boat, fridge, bike, board." Then two things happened at once. Firstly, she saw, protruding from the rushing debris, a white, lifeless foot. Secondly, she remembered Sarah that morning. "Matt and I are going diving for the day. Wanna come?" She closed her eyes and inhaled the deepest breath of her life.

She looked at Noah. He was repeating something in his mother tongue. Over and over again like the Buddhist chants broadcast at sunrise over the hillside. As her eyes accustomed to the sight, her other senses snapped to attention. She felt her shoulders prickle with heat. She tasted blood and realised she'd been biting her bottom lip. She pushed her palm to her nose to protect it from the rising stench of boiling saltwater. Of the hell's symphony orchestra in full swing, the note that would stay with Talitha for years to come, rousing her from a clammy slumber again and again, was the distress call of a peacock, standing proud atop a floating thatched roof, still intact but detached from the beach shack it was designed to crown. She looked at Noah. "I need to go," she said. "Come with me?"

"I stay," he replied. She squeezed his arm and left.

The hostel, perched between a tea plantation and The People's Bank of Sri Lanka, was silent. She found Aaron in the back office, feet up on the sofa with a spliff, watching the portable bracketed to the wall. BBC Worldwide was announcing reports of a tidal wave hitting a stretch of coastline in Thailand but they had no other information at that time. Aaron moved his feet so Talitha could sit down. She took a long drag on the spliff he held out to her. An iced-over runway was causing major delays at Charles de Gaulle Airport. An angry Parisian told a reporter he still had no idea if he'd be flying anytime soon, such was the appalling lack of communication by his airline. Meanwhile, an unprecedented number of UK shoppers had been queuing since five o'clock that morning to be among the first to snap up Boxing Day bargains at Lakeside. Over on Sky, a shaky handheld camera recorded the futile attempts of a crowd to run from the wave bearing down on them. SUMATRA DEATH TOLL RISES ran the banner at the bottom of the screen. The newscaster read out the email address to which eyewitnesses could send their home footage.

Talitha turned on the fan in Matt and Sarah's room. Picked a towel off the floor and hung it over a hook on the back of the door. Made the bed. Swept the condom wrapper into the wastepaper basket. Sat. And waited.

She must have fallen asleep. She shivered against the breeze from the whirring fan and felt along the wall for the light. It was midday. Aaron was in the same spot, snoring with three spliffs stubbed out in the ashtray balancing precariously on his thigh. She moved it to the table and muted the television.

Other guests began to trickle in. None were hungry or thirsty but Talitha made pots of tea and a tray of sandwiches anyway. One, a Londoner, had been told that their embassy required British citizens to register immediately; a Russian girl surmised that all embassies were probably putting out the same call, and that they should also alert the relevant embassies to anyone missing. Aaron, bleary-eyed, was checking off names against his logbook. Everyone was accounted for, he said. With two exceptions. Nobody looked at Talitha.

She went to her room and dug out her passport and

insurance papers, went to Matt and Sarah's and looked around for theirs. Matt had long hair in his photo. Sarah had two passports. One Australian, one British. She hadn't mentioned the fact of her dual citizenship. She returned to the lounge, hoping to accompany the Londoner to the embassy, but he'd left already.

She had anticipated chaos; queues of weeping holidaymakers headed by unblinking officials. But there were just a few groups milling about, talking in hushed, reverential tones. Somewhere a phone was ringing. She spotted the Londoner. He caught her eye and turned to a middle-aged woman who glanced at Talitha as he said something in her ear. The woman was coming towards her now. "Sarah?" she asked. Talitha nodded. "She went diving. Early this morning. I brought her ID." When the woman left Talitha she realised she'd been addressing her as Sarah, not asking about her whereabouts. "I'll leave you with Azor," the woman said, returning with a young guy who looked local but spoke BBC English. "I need you to fill in these forms: one for you and one for your friend," he said. "It shouldn't take long. Do you have her passport?" She put her head in her hands and sank her elbows into her knees. Azor took her passport, flipped to the photo page and scribbled something on his hand in biro. "Here you go. It really won't take long," he promised.

The forms required block capitals, black ink, full names, passport numbers, places and dates of birth. "That was quick," Azor said when he returned a few minutes later to see how she was getting on. "You're doing great." He nodded as he checked the forms against the passports. He handed one back and secured the other under the clasp of his clipboard.

"Sarah," she heard a name shout after her. "Wait up." It was the Londoner. She still didn't know his name and hadn't the energy to correct him. "Here, let me take that for you," he said, swinging her bag over his shoulder. He put his arm around her and led her back to the hostel. She went straight to Sarah's room, pulled back the shutters and lay down in darkness.

But she couldn't sleep. She turned on the lamp and felt in her bag for the passport. She didn't have to open it to know it wasn't hers. The golden crest on Sarah's cover was worn, the corners better thumbed.

Sarah must have taken her wallet on the boat, but her handful of cards, among them a VISA, driving licence, an organ donor card and her PADI certification, was tucked between the pages of the paperback she was a quarter way through, a chick lit novel with a neon-pink cover. Talitha stared at the ceiling and waited to fall into what would be a mercifully dreamless sleep.

She looked up at the departure board. Gate 4 was flashing. "Could all remaining passengers on United Emirates flight 654 to Hong Kong International please proceed immediately to Gate 4, where your flight is ready for boarding."

As she removed Sarah's sandals to pass through security, Talitha glanced back at the concourse. A smiling woman was balancing a toddler on her hip and encouraging his clenched fist back and fore like windshield wipers in the direction of the man passing through the scanner up ahead. He looked back and smiled. Raised his hand to return the gesture. "Say goodbye now, baby," the woman urged. "Wave goodbye."

Notes

1) Zoologists have hypothesised that elephants are able to sense the seismic vibrations of earthquakes long before humans can. On the morning of 26th December 2004, a herd of elephants in Thailand began to make strange noises and tugged free of their restraints, escaping to higher ground before the "Boxing Day tsunami" hit the shore. (Reported in *Tsunami: Anatomy Of A Disaster*, March 2005, http://news.bbc.co.uk/1/hi/sci/tech/4381395.stm)

"Our perfect companions never have fewer than four feet."

Colette, Sidonie-Gabrielle - novelist, 1873 – 1954

A LOVERS TALE
Angela Songui

The Crocodile
The Heron stood on the far shore, her reflection in the still waters made a twinned glory of her long legs and powerful breast. I
watched from the reeds, trying not to breathe or disturb the quiet of
the waters that morning. She bent her long elegant neck towards the
surface, to kiss perhaps what I knew I'd grow to adore. Instead, in a
flash of precise movement she withdrew, a silver fish wriggling on
the tip of her regal beak.
For all of my practice and patience I could never move as she, for I
dwell under the liquid glaze or on a sunny bank, never in between.
Often I would come to her and keeping a respectful distance I would
sing to her the contents of my heart.
In daylight she stood grandly above the rest, a frank and watchful
eye ever-darting, a thin smile stretched pleasantly across her lips.
The reeds and bulrushes bent in a dance around her, catching the
wind at play in her virginal feathers.
I waited.
The night brought her to the edge of the shore. Her footprints sunk
and filled with stars; waters slid off her back in silver beads and
soundlessly rejoined the gently swirling currents.
I love uncontrollably; she had a beauty unmeasured that my heart
ached to know and possess. And so I sang.
I sang of the deep and the centuries, I sang of lost lovers and broken
men. And I waited – I watched and waited.

The Snowy Heron
As he approached I was frightened. I'll admit this fact. But the racing of my heart soon gave way to a rushing in my blood. I couldn't

help it – it's primordial, you see.

Long have I been drawn to such power; the armoured muscles of his back, the certainty of his grin.

He sang to me from the reeds, high and sweet, and did this daily when I ventured out for my breakfast. Sometimes he would sing for hours and then sit himself on a sandy bank and shed tears. Often he entreated me to come nearer, to end his torment, to love him as he loved me.

At night, he came to the surface, a slice of flat dense blackness around which the moon ran rings and danced and shone like ribbons of pure white. This was his halo. This made him beautiful. His voice travelled across the quivering pools and into my pin-prick ears whispering musical passions that moved me hypnotically.

His life for mine, he said, laying bare his rude armour at my feet. His smile lasted a lifetime and was for me alone. So this is Love.

Brushing his jawbone with the delicate tips of my wings I drew him to me. The desire was too much, the want greater still. I offered myself to his song, his night and his kiss. The sighs we chorused into the air made the birds lift from the trees nearby.

Together

She opened her vast wings to encompass him and accepted without protest his embrace. His kiss – he clamped his weight upon her, pried her love apart. She burst the night open with her cries, the thrumming of her feathers in graceful fruitless flight. Her head bent to his, necks entwined unashamed of their engagement.

His heart grew to bursting in his mighty chest and she covered his face with her wings so as not to see his tears. No tears tonight, just the two coming together - each hunger fed. Taking his delicate lady in his vice he drew her down and down; over each other they rolled innocent and complete. Her neck a strand of graceful sea grass flowing with the currents out towards a nameless ocean.

The Authors Gratefully Acknowledge

Ruggiero Campopiano at Picsoul - for the layout, design, patience and unending encouragement
www.picsoul.com

Josephine Dexter – for the cover illustration artwork and imaginary places

The London School of Journalism - for getting us inspired, and getting us together
www.lsj.org

Neil Andrew Taylor, author, playwright and poet – for giving of his time & talents as a teacher and writer
www.neilandrewtaylor.co.uk

Lucy Caldwell, novelist and award-winning playwright – for all the knowledge shared in her 'advanced' tutorials at LSJ

XTFX Limited, purveyors of the finest in VFX solutions - for the space and support
www.xtfx.co.uk

Edwin Law - for his continued support

The staff at The Mayhew Animal Home – for their enthusiastic support of our initiative

In their 125th year of operation, **The Mayhew Animal Home** continues to provide a much-needed service sheltering and caring for London's unwanted or discarded domestic animals. For one and a quarter centuries The Mayhew has been a refuge to the voiceless thousands, sadly in need and in want of a home.
Always ready with a friendly, gentle touch, the shelter's staff work with tireless care and compassion, ensuring that their dogs, cats and rabbits have the best opportunity of finding a loving companion.

To further assist **The Mayhew** in their efforts, or to find out how you can volunteer, visit their website at: www.mayhewanimalhome.org

AUTHOR BIOGRAPHIES

Amarpreet Basi
Amarpreet splits his time between New York and Paris. That's a lie. In reality, Amarpreet is an invertebrate wage slave chained to a desk in Canary Wharf. His first book, Will I Ever Get Published?, has yet to be published. His second book isn't really a book but a pipe-dream masquerading as an ambition wrapped up in a membrane of risible delusion. In his spare time, Amarpreet enjoys having black-and-white photographs taken of himself whilst looking thoughtful and introspective with his chin resting on his fist.

Amy Blyth
Amy lives in East London with her partner and also her pet rat Ruby. She has always been passionate about books, films and writing and hopes to one day complete her very own post-apocalyptic novel. A film studies graduate and journalism MA, Amy now works full-time writing content for a home improvements publication.

Josephine Dexter
At some innocuous point in 2004 Josephine realized that writing was her way forward. At the same moment the phrase 'situations change' entered her mind. These words have been a guiding force ever since. A woodland creature at heart, she now lives in London and is working on her first novel. Since completing two writing courses at LSJ, Josephine has written several short stories.

Rebecca Jenkins
Rebecca Jenkins was born and grew up in South Wales and studied German Literature at the University of Swansea. Since moving to London in 2000 she has worked as a journalist, copy writer, editor and website manager for entertainment brands and women's maga-zines. She lives in Hertfordshire and is currently working on a novel.

WTA Mackewn

WTA Mackewn recently joined a gym. After turning 30 he realised that his once underweight boyish athleticism was a thing of the past and decided it was time to get fit. After an enthusiastic start with a Brazilian personal trainer, his motivation soon lapsed and he now spends most of his time feeling guilty about not going. Three Twats and a Dog Turd is his response to all the morons he has to cater to during his working day in Soho. His aim with the story is that some of them read the work, realise the error of their ways and move to remote parts of Scotland under a cloud of shame. Other than that, he lives with his wife and cat in Wandsworth.

Angela Songui

After fully complying with DEFRA regulations, Angela's cats, Tiger and Osee successfully imported their biped from Montreal, Canada to London in 2008, where they continue to enjoy the benefits of her opposable thumbs and chin-rubbing abilities and encourage her to write for tuna. Angela and her British partner, James, function nicely as can-openers, are relatively low-maintenance and have good grooming habits. Angela is an event producer and sometimes misses Montreal bagels.

Christina Thompson

Christina Thompson loves all forms of storytelling. Her love of travel has opened up a curiosity for myths, legends and folklore from all over the world. Some of her most memorable dreams have been steeped in animal lore. She frequently talks to the living creatures she encounters on her daily wanderings. In recent years, she has discovered a great passion for the ukulele. She lives in Montreal, Canada.

Neil Andrew Taylor

Neil Andrew Taylor is a successful author and playwright based in London. His adaptations of British screen classics and novels have been widely performed nationally in the UK, including runs on Shaftesbury Avenue, in London's West-End. His world premier works include stage versions of Room at the Top, Kind Hearts and Coronets, The Lady Vanishes, and Noel Coward's Brief Encounter, and many others. He lectures internationally on Creative Writing and writing for theatre and film, and also performs as a prose poet.